He would still bed her tonight

But having Nicole Power mindless with desire for him would be an added bonus. How brilliantly satisfying that would be!

His hand moved and his fingers found their goal.

Her nipple was hard, like a river pebble.

"No, don't," she whimpered.

He ignored her protest and bent his head to put his mouth where his fingertip had been. There was absolutely no pretense in her responses. She was his, to do with as he pleased. His to explore and exploit. His to win and maybe even to wed.

Did he want to go that far? Did he want to see her walk down the aisle in white? Did he want to see blind adoration as well as the mindless desire he'd just glimpsed in her beautiful green eyes?

There was only one answer to those questions.

An unequivocal yes.

Three Rich
HUSBANDS

*When a wealthy man takes a wife,
it's not always for love...*

Meet Russell, Hugh and James, three wealthy
Sydney businessmen who've been the best of
friends for ages. They know each other very
well—including the reasons none of them
believe in marrying for love.

While Russell and Hugh have so far remained
single, James is about to embark on his second
marriage.

But all this is set to change as Russell and Hugh
are also driven to the altar. Have they changed
their minds about love—or are they ruthlessly
making marriages of convenience?

Find out in Miranda Lee's sizzling, breathtaking,
daring new trilogy, out this fall!

Book one:
The Billionaire's Bride of Vengeance
(September)

Book two:
The Billionaire's Bride of Convenience
(October)

Book three:
The Billionaire's Bride of Innocence
(November)

Miranda Lee

THE BILLIONAIRE'S BRIDE OF VENGEANCE

Three Rich
HUSBANDS

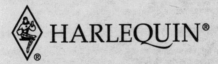

HARLEQUIN®

TORONTO • NEW YORK • LONDON
AMSTERDAM • PARIS • SYDNEY • HAMBURG
STOCKHOLM • ATHENS • TOKYO • MILAN • MADRID
PRAGUE • WARSAW • BUDAPEST • AUCKLAND

ISBN-13: 978-0-373-12852-5

THE BILLIONAIRE'S BRIDE OF VENGEANCE

First North American Publication 2009.

Copyright © 2008 by Miranda Lee.

All about the author...
Miranda Lee

MIRANDA LEE was born in Port Macquarie, a popular
seaside town on the mid-north coast of New South
Wales, Australia, and is the youngest of four children.
Her father was a country schoolteacher and brilliant
sportsman. Her mother was a talented dressmaker.

After leaving her convent school, Miranda briefly
studied the cello before moving to Sydney, where she
embraced the emerging world of computers. Her career
as a programmer ended after she married, had three
daughters and bought a small acreage in a semirural
community.

Following this, Miranda attempted greyhound training,
as well as horse and goat breeding, but was left
dissatisfied. She yearned to find a creative career from
which she could earn money. When her sister suggested
writing romances, it seemed like a good idea. She could
do it at home, and it might even be fun!

It took a decade of trial and error before her first
romance, *After the Affair,* was accepted and published.
At that time, Miranda, her husband and her three
daughters had moved back to the central coast, where
they could enjoy the sun and the surf lifestyle once again.

Bravely, her husband left his executive position to stay
home and support Miranda's career. He learned to cook
and to clean, two invaluable household skills.

Numerous successful stories followed, each embodying
Miranda's trademark style: fast-paced and sexy rhythms;
passionate, real-life characters; and enduring, memorable
story lines. She has one credo when writing romances:
Don't bore the reader! Millions of fans worldwide agree
she never does.

PROLOGUE

RUSSELL'S hands tightened on the steering wheel as he arrived at the address he'd been given.

'Mr Power is out of the office today,' he'd been told when he burst into Power Mortgages half an hour earlier and demanded to see Alistair Power.

At first the receptionist had refused to tell Russell where Power might be, no doubt sensing trouble in the eyes of the distraught young man standing in front of her desk. But Russell's ironically truthful statement that he had urgent business with her boss concerning the tragic death of a business associate had finally elicited the information he wanted. Mr Power and his wife were at the construction site of their new home in the exclusive Sydney suburb of Belleview Hill.

Russell had somehow managed a smile and the girl had jotted down the address.

He wasn't smiling now, a bitter bile filling his mouth as he stared up at what was obviously going to be a grand mansion. Amazing what one could buy with other people's money!

Russell wrenched the wheel of his rusty old car towards the gravel driveway and drove right up to the front of the three-storeyed building. The shell of the house was finished, the roof was on, the front steps in place. A middle-aged man in a superbly tailored business suit was standing up on the porch, a leggy blonde next to him.

Power's trophy wife, obviously.

Russell didn't stop to think, his emotions spilling over at the sight of the man whose greed had driven his father to despair and suicide. Hatred propelled him out of the car, his hands curling into furious fists as he charged up the steps.

'Alistair Power!' he called out at the same time.

Cool grey eyes raked over him; Power was not overly perturbed, it seemed, by Russell's aggressive approach.

'Yes. Can I help you?'

Russell could not believe the man's lack of concern. Couldn't he see his visitor had murder in his heart?

Russell resisted the urge to punch Power then and there. First, he wanted the creep to know who he was and why he'd come.

'I thought you'd like to know that my father killed himself last week.'

Power's eyebrows arched. 'And your father is?'

'Keith McClain.'

'That name means nothing to me. I know no Keith McClain.'

My God, he didn't even recognise his father's name! Yet Russell knew that his dad—his shy but proud dad—had gone to Power personally and begged him for more time to repay his loan.

'You knew him well enough to let him take out two mortgages on his farm,' Russell ground out, 'when he had no possible means of meeting the repayments. He had no stock, no crops, no income. The ten-year drought had seen to that. But his land was valuable, wasn't it? So you deliberately let him get into debt and then you just took it!'

'Young man, I don't force people to take out mortgages.'

'You shouldn't agree to lend money which you know people can't pay back,' Russell countered heatedly. 'I've made some enquiries about Power Mortgages and that's your *modus operandi*.'

Power didn't bat an eyelid. 'I haven't done anything illegal. The mistake was your father's. He should have sold his property rather than borrow more money.'

'But the land had been in his family for generations! He knew nothing else but farming.'

'That's not my fault.'

'But it *is* your fault. You, and men like you. You don't have any feelings, any compassion. All you care about is making money.'

'Business has little room for compassion, son.'

'Don't you call me son, you greedy bastard,' Russell snapped, a red haze of grief launching him forwards.

The trophy wife threw herself in front of Power, stopping Russell in his tracks.

'Don't!' she cried, her hands fluttering up to ward off Russell's fists. 'It'll only make things worse. And it won't bring your father back.'

He stared into her striking green eyes and saw she didn't really have any compassion, either. She was just protecting her lifestyle.

The seeds of a different vengeance were sown in Russell at that point; a vengeance which would be far more satisfying than murder.

Pulling away from her, Russell whirled and walked back down the steps. At the bottom, he turned and glared back up at Power.

'One day,' he threatened, his eyes as hard as his heart, 'one day, I'm going to destroy you. I vow on my father's grave that I won't rest till I take everything you hold dear, the way you took everything from him!'

CHAPTER ONE

Sixteen years later...

BANGKOK WAS HOT, VERY hot. And humid.

By the time Nicole had walked the kilometre from her cheap hotel to the orphanage, her singlet top was clinging to her back.

The Nicole of a few months ago would have complained incessantly about her limp-rag hair and sweaty clothes. If she'd been staying in Bangkok back then, she would not have moved from her five-star, air-conditioned hotel, except to take a dip in the pool, or a ride in a luxury limousine.

But that Nicole no longer existed. On one traumatic day last June, her very spoiled eyes had been opened by the discovery that the three main people in her life were not the good guys she'd believed them to be.

First, she'd walked in on her soon-to-be husband having sex on his office desk with his PA. Neither of them had noticed her presence in the doorway at the time.

Shattered, Nicole had fled home to her mother who'd amazingly tried to convince her that it was impossible for wealthy, successful men to be faithful. If Nicole was sensible, she'd learn to turn a blind eye to her fiancé's sexual transgressions.

'I always do whenever Alistair strays,' her mother had said without turning a hair on her beautifully coiffured blonde head.

The realisation that her stepfather had been sleeping around, and that her mother collaborated with his adultery, had shocked Nicole, possibly even more than David's infidelity.

It had all been too much. A pampered princess she might have become since her mother married Alistair, but she was not without morals or feelings.

The following day she'd returned her engagement ring, resulting in an argument during which David had said some cutting things to her about her inadequacies in the bedroom. After that she'd had an equally unpleasant confrontation with her stepfather, who'd called her naïve and narrow-minded.

'The winners in this world don't always follow the rules,' he'd stated arrogantly. 'David is a winner. As his wife, you, my dear Nicole, could have had it all. Now I'll have to find you another rich husband who can keep you in the manner to which you've become accustomed.'

Nicole had been rendered speechless by the inference that David had been procured for her by her stepfather.

But, with hindsight, she realised that had probably been so.

Nicole had immediately quit her totally superficial and no doubt nepotistically acquired position in the PR department of Power Mortgages. That same afternoon, she'd answered an ad in a newspaper to go on a backpacking holiday with another girl whose friend had withdrawn from the trip at the last minute. A week later

Nicole had flown out of Mascot Airport with nothing but her severance pay, hopeful of finding some much needed independence, plus some new priorities other than the supposed good things in life.

Now, four months later, she was a different person.

A real person, she liked to think, living in the real world.

'Nicoe, Nicoe!' the children at the orphanage chorused when she walked into the dusty compound where they were playing.

Nicole smiled at how they couldn't pronounce the letter 'l'. Yet on the whole their English was very good, courtesy of the wonderful woman who ran the orphanage.

After hugs and kisses all round, the children begged her to sing something for them. Music had always been a great love of Nicole's and she had a good voice.

'What song would you like?' she asked, hooking her carry-all over her shoulder and heading for the shade of the only tree that graced the yard.

'Warzing Matinda!' a little boy called out.

'"Waltzing Matilda", you mean,' she said, ruffling his thick black hair.

'Yes, Nicoe. Warzing Matinda.'

She laughed, and they all laughed, too. It always amazed Nicole how happy these children could be. Yet, materially speaking, they had nothing. She'd thought she'd been poor before her mother had met and married Alistair. Compared to these orphans, she'd been rich.

'All right. Let's sit down here.'

The kids all settled down in the dirt under the tree, their eager faces turned up towards her.

Nicole opened her mouth and began to sing.

'"Once a jolly swagman camped by a billabong,
Under the shade of a coolabah tree.

And he sang as he watched and waited till his billy boiled.

You'll come a-waltzing Matilda with me…'''

None of the children moved a muscle till she finished the famous Australian ballad, after which they jumped up and clapped and begged her to sing it again. She would have, if the chime on her cellphone hadn't interrupted.

'Excuse me,' she said as she fished out her phone from her bag. 'Off you go and play for a while.'

Nicole already suspected who might be calling. Her mother rang her every week, all the while pretending that her daughter wasn't disgusted with her. Nicole didn't have the heart to cut the woman out of her life entirely. She still loved her mother, and knew her mother loved her.

'Yes?' she answered.

'Nicole, it's your mother.'

Nicole frowned. Something was wrong. Her mother never called herself that. On top of which, her voice sounded very strained.

'Hello, Mum. What's up?'

'I…um…' Mrs Power broke off, then suddenly blurted out, 'You have to come home.'

Nicole's frown deepened. 'Come home? Why?' She paused. 'Mum, where are you?'

'I can't tell you that.'

'What? Why not?'

'Your father doesn't want anyone to know where we are.'

'Alistair Power is not my father,' Nicole said coldly.

'He's more of a father than that married creep who impregnated me,' her mother snapped. 'Alistair, no! Let me talk to her.'

Nicole heard the sound of a scuffle in the background.

'Now you listen to me, you ungrateful little chit!' Alistair spat out down the line. 'If it had been up to me, I wouldn't have bothered with this call. But your mother loves you, though lord knows why. This is the situation. My company has gone belly-up and my creditors are baying for more blood, so we've left Australia for good. The bank has repossessed the house in Belleview Hill and no doubt will sell it, lock, stock and barrel, to some greedy opportunist.'

'But…but all my things are still there!' Nicole protested.

'That's why your mother called. To tell you to get your butt back to Sydney pronto before the locks are changed and all your personal possessions are sent to a charity or the rubbish tip.'

'They can't do that!'

'Who's to stop them? I certainly can't.'

Nicole groaned. She didn't give a damn about her designer clothes. But she did care about all the mementos of her childhood, especially her school days, which had been very happy. There were several photo albums and scrapbooks which were irreplaceable to her. That they might be thrown into some skip filled her with horror.

'Here's your mother again,' Alistair growled.

'You don't have to worry about your jewellery, dear,' her mother said in a sugary-sweet voice. 'I brought it all with me.'

'I don't care about the jewellery, Mum.'

'But it's worth a small fortune!'

She was right, Nicole realised. Her stepfather had showered her with beautiful pieces over the years: diamonds, pearls and lots of emeralds.

'To match your beautiful eyes,' he'd said more than once, ladling on the false charm which came so easily to him.

It suddenly occurred to Nicole that if she sold her jewellery, she would have the funds to make some much needed improvements to this orphanage. It would be silly to throw such an opportunity away for the sake of pride.

'Would it be possible for you to send my jewellery to me, Mum?'

'Of course. But where? Every time I ring you, you're in a different country. Which one is it now?'

'The same one as last time. Thailand. On second thoughts, could you courier all my jewellery to Kara's place? I'll let her know it's coming. You remember her address, don't you?'

'How could I possibly forget? I drove you there enough times. You are going home, then, to collect your things?'

'Yes. As soon as I can get a flight to Sydney.' Thank goodness she already had a pre-paid return ticket, because she was almost broke.

'That's good. It really bothered me, having to leave behind all those lovely clothes of yours.'

Nicole sighed. *Glad to see you've still got your priorities right, Mum.*

'I'm sorry I can't tell you where we are. But you don't have to worry,' her mother whispered down the line. 'We have plenty of money to live on. Alistair deposited a good chunk into an offshore account last year. If you need anything, you only have to ask.'

Nicole shuddered. *Over my dead body.* 'I should go, Mum.'

'Ring me from Sydney, won't you?'

'OK.'

Nicole shook her head as she hung up. There was no hope for her mother, she realised sadly. No hope at all.

CHAPTER TWO

TOTAL revenge, Russell was forced to accept as he drove towards his enemy's mansion in Bellevue Hill, was very difficult to achieve.

For sixteen years, the thought of vengeance had sustained him as he'd worked tirelessly to create the means to bring down the man who'd been responsible for his father's death. To make Power pay for what he'd done—not just to Russell's father, but to thousands of other desperate people.

At last the opportunity had presented itself, courtesy of the meltdown of the prime mortgage market in the USA. Russell had gone in for the kill, ruthlessly selling all the shares in Power Mortgages that he'd secretly acquired over the years. In one short week, he'd succeeded in wiping millions off that amoral bastard's fortune.

When Sydney's real estate grapevine—to which Russell was privy—revealed that Power had borrowed extensively to support his lavish lifestyle, and that his banker had repossessed his multi-million dollar mansion, Russell had made an immediate offer for the house which he'd known would not be refused. He hadn't bothered with an inspection of the building, or with viewing the contents, which were part of the deal. He hadn't wanted to set foot in the place till it was his.

And now he was on his way there, the contracts safely signed, the keys in his pocket.

He should have been over the moon.

But he wasn't.

Why?

Because the bastard had escaped, that's why. Fled the country, flown off to some secret overseas hideaway, where he'd probably funnelled millions into off-shore accounts so that he wouldn't have to pay back his many creditors in Australia.

The thought of Alistair Power lying back on some beach in the Bahamas irked Russell no end. Men like that had no right to live, let alone live in the lap of luxury.

Still, there was some satisfaction to be gained from knowing that his enemy's reputation had been ruined. No longer would Power be fêted by presidents and prime ministers. Nor would that smarmy smile of his be continuously flashed across television screens, because of coverage of whatever super-glamorous party he happened to be throwing that weekend.

The venue for those parties came into view. Russell finally saw the finished version of the three-storeyed mansion he'd visited that fateful day sixteen years earlier.

An hour ago, he'd been listening to the man handling the sale at the bank wax lyrical about how the house had been designed to take full advantage of its site on one of the highest points in Bellevue Hill: how each floor had lots of terraces and balconies, all with wonderful views of the city and harbour; how the top level was devoted entirely to living rooms, providing the perfect setting for parties.

But no verbal description could do justice to the visual impact of the building, with its dazzlingly white cement-rendered walls and the rich, royal-blue trim around its many windows and doors.

Russell pulled into the driveway and braked to a halt in front of a pair of security gates.

Sixteen years ago, there'd been no security at all. In fact, there'd been nothing to stop him from doing what he'd gone here to do.

Russell sighed.

Part of him would always regret that he'd settled for vengeful words that day, rather than actions. Still, if he had given in to his violent urgings, he'd be currently looking through prison bars and not the wrought-iron ones in front of him. He certainly wouldn't be sitting here in a rich man's car, wearing a rich man's suit.

Russell pressed the remote he'd been given, waiting with learned patience till the gates swung open, after which he drove slowly around the circular drive that surrounded a magnificent marble Italian-style fountain.

Russell bypassed the six-car garage at the side of the house, parking his racing-green Aston Martin at the base of the flight of stone steps which led up to a now impressively columned front porch. With the house keys in his hand, he climbed out from behind the wheel then walked up the steps, stopping once he reached the top to turn round and take in the view.

The grounds were as magnificent as the fountain, having the grandeur which would have befitted a palace, with extensive lawns edged with perfectly pruned hedges and perfectly placed shade trees. Russell had been assured that the back garden was more impressive than the front, with a large terrace, a solar-heated pool and a synthetic-surface tennis court.

'The pool has a pool house,' the man at the bank had rattled on, 'which has its own kitchen, bathroom, two guest bedrooms and a spacious living area. It's larger than a lot of Sydney apartments.'

Possibly larger than his own, Russell accepted. He currently lived quite modestly in a two-bedroom unit on McMahon's Point, having never felt the need for anything bigger, or more opulent. After all, he only went there to eat and sleep. Unlike a lot of successful real-estate agents, he didn't entertain much. When he did, it was never at home.

Power's mansion, however, was not the kind of home one only slept in. It was built for showing off…built as a monument to its owner's material success.

And now it was all his.

Once again, Russell didn't experience the rush of triumphant pleasure he'd always anticipated such a moment would bring. Was it a case of the journey being better than reaching the destination? Or was it that he had no one to share his vengeance with?

His mother had never succumbed to the anger and bitterness which had consumed Russell after his father's suicide. She hadn't blamed Power Mortgages at all, astonishing Russell with the revelation that his father had suffered from depression for some time, which had led to the poor decisions that had resulted in their farm being repossessed. She'd dismissed the fact that Power Mortgages specialised in arranging loans for people who had no hope of repaying them in the first place.

After grieving for her much-loved husband for a

couple of years, Frieda McClain had chosen to move on with her life, marrying another farmer.

Russell had never been able to understand his mother's attitude. Frankly, he'd felt almost betrayed by the briefness of her mourning. He'd been absolutely devastated by his father's suicide, his sorrow made all the worse by a measure of guilt.

Russell hated the thought that one of the reasons his father had borrowed so much had been to give his son the kind of education he'd never received himself. Although Russell had won a scholarship to a top Sydney boarding school, of course there'd been more expenses involved than just the fees. Then, after Russell had passed his high-school certificate, his father had insisted he go on to uni, paying for him to share a flat with his much wealthier school friends, even buying him an old car to get around in.

He should have known his dad couldn't afford any of it. He should have seen the truth behind the white lies. The evidence had been there every time he went home.

Russell had been close to suicide himself the day he'd buried his father.

Only the thought of revenge had sustained him, giving him something to live for. After his run-in with Power he'd immediately dropped out of his law degree and taken a job as a real-estate salesman, luckily finding a position in a premier agency in Sydney's exclusive eastern suburbs. Over the next few years, he'd spent a lot less time with his friends—and even less with girls—channelling all his energies into becoming rich enough to have the weapons to ruin Alistair Power.

At the age of thirty-six, he was Sydney's most suc-cessful real-estate agent, owning several businesses in the best Sydney suburbs, plus a personal portfolio of property to rival the wealthiest in Australia, a portfolio which now included one of Sydney's most photographed homes.

Russell realised, as he turned and strode under the covered portico, that the media were sure to get hold of the news that he'd bought this place. Such purchases were news. For a split-second, he considered doing what he'd never done before: give an interview to a journalist in the vain hope that Power might read it and finally connect the Russell McClain of McClain Real Estate with that long-haired youth who'd threatened vengeance all those years ago.

Waste of time, Russell decided as he slotted the key into the brass lock of the double front doors. Because Power wouldn't make the connection. They'd already met again—over a property deal—and there'd not been a hint of recognition in Power's face. It seemed men without consciences didn't remember their victims for long. Possibly because there were too many of them.

What a cold-blooded bastard!

As Russell pushed open the heavy front doors and stepped into the cavernous foyer of the house, a surprising sound met his ears.

Singing.

Startled, he stood stock-still and listened.

Yes. Someone was singing somewhere upstairs—a woman.

Russell frowned. Could it be a radio, perhaps left playing by the cleaning service which the bank said had serviced the place yesterday?

No, it wasn't a radio, he quickly deduced, the voice having no instrumental backing.

Someone was in his house, someone who shouldn't be there. And they were upstairs, singing.

Russell knew exactly who it was.

A squatter.

It was a scenario not unfamiliar to him.

People would be amazed at how often empty homes were squatted in, even ones as lavish as this. It didn't matter how much security you had, how high the walls were or how many locks you had—these street-smart scroungers found a way in.

Russell planned his course of action as he made his way quietly up the curving staircase to the first floor.

Often there was a whole group of them, usually junkies. Sometimes, however, it was just some runaway looking for a place to sleep. Or to shower.

He suspected this might be the latter.

When Russell reached the first landing, he could hear the faint hiss of water running as well as the singing. It sounded as if she *was* in the shower. He moved across the wide, carpeted landing to the door straight in front of him. Very carefully, he turned the knob and popped his head in.

No, not in here, Russell quickly deduced.

He shook his head as he glanced around what had to be the master bedroom. Power certainly hadn't stinted on the decor. Even if the French-style furniture was reproduction, it must still have cost a packet. So had the movie-size television screen built into the wall opposite the foot of the bed.

Russell's eyebrows lifted. Maybe twenty million was a bargain price for this place. The contents alone were worth a small fortune. It must have hurt Power to leave it all behind.

He sure as hell hoped so.

It pained him that Power would probably never know who had bought his house. It pained him even more that he would never be able to have a more personal revenge on the man.

Maybe he would gain some more satisfaction when he actually moved in, which he fully intended to do tomorrow.

But, first, he had to turf out his unwelcome guest.

Shutting the door, he moved along the corridor to his left where he popped his head in the next door.

It was another bedroom, very pretty and very feminine.

The queen-sized bed had obviously been slept in, the gold satin quilt thrown back, the pillows crumpled.

The sound of water running was definitely louder in there, though the singing had suddenly stopped. Slipping inside, Russell made his way silently across the room, noting the bundle of cheap-looking clothes thrown carelessly on the floor next to the bed.

He shook his head at the sight. The hide of this woman!

When he reached what he presumed was the bathroom door he considered knocking first, but decided against giving this bold interloper any warning.

Too bad if she was stark naked, he decided angrily as he reached for the door knob. Squatters didn't deserve any consideration or respect.

Without thinking of the possible consequences of his actions, Russell turned the knob and pushed open the door.

CHAPTER THREE

SHE *was* naked, with the kind of body which took a man's breath away: tall and slender, with long legs, perfect breasts and a pert but curvy little bottom.

She didn't notice him standing there, her eyes squeezed tightly shut as she vigorously shampooed her long, fair hair.

Russell made no move to make his presence known to her. He was way too busy admiring the view. Yet he'd never been the kind of man to openly ogle women, or to salivate over centrefolds.

But he was on the verge of salivating now, not to mention succumbing to an increasingly forbidden fantasy.

Perhaps he'd been too long without a woman...

On the whole, Russell didn't find his mainly celibate lifestyle too much of a hardship. Working twenty-four-seven absorbed his energies to a large degree. But at least once a month his male hormones would rebel.

Despite not being traditionally handsome, Russell never had any trouble attracting women, especially when he put himself in an environment conducive to seduction. Sydney nightclubs always had a plethora of beautiful young things who were only too willing and eager to accommodate him, first on the dance floor and then in his bed.

Possibly, some of these girls had hoped things would progress beyond the kind of brief, strictly sexual liaisons Russell indulged in, despite his always having made it clear right from the start that it wouldn't.

And it never did. Relationships were definitely not on Russell's agenda. Never had been, never would be. Something had happened to his heart after his father's death: it had lost the capacity to love and to trust. His heart had become hard, he knew.

However, another part of Russell's body was hard at this precise moment.

Frustration raged as he continued to look at the naked nymph in the shower. Frustration, plus the wickedest of temptations.

When her hands lifted to smooth her soapy hair back from her forehead, she tipped her face up into the spray, turning it this way and that.

Russell's fascinated gaze fastened on her face. She was beautiful, with delicate features and clear skin. Of course, he couldn't see her eyes, which remained tightly shut. But it seemed impossible that Mother Nature could have fashioned a creature so lovely, then given her ugly eyes.

No, they would be beautiful, like the rest of her.

Once she opened them, however, and saw him standing there, staring at her, all hell would break loose. She would probably scream the place down.

I should have called the police and not burst in here, Russell realised with hindsight.

Experience had taught him that squatters and runaways were extremely wily. If he called the police now, he wouldn't put it past this girl to concoct some story that he'd invited her here. She might even cry rape. And they just might believe her, given her looks.

Russell did the only thing he could, under the circumstances. He backed out of the room, shutting the door very quietly behind him. There he waited till the shower was turned off and sufficient time had passed for her to have dried and dressed herself.

Then he did the right thing.

He knocked.

'Who is it?' the girl called out.

'More to the point, who are you?' he challenged.

'Nicole Power,' she called back.

'Who?' Had he heard right? Had she really said she was Nicole Power? Surely not!

'Nicole Power,' she repeated.

Shock rendered Russell speechless.

Nicole Power! Of all people! Of all *women*!

He hadn't recognised her. Not without her clothes on, and not without her eyes open.

Even worse was the fact that he'd fancied her. No, that was an understatement. He'd *lusted* after her, with a force that was as blind as it was almost overpowering.

For a moment back there in that bathroom, when he'd believed she was a penniless runaway, he'd imagined making her an offer that was as wrong as it was wickedly exciting.

'You can stay,' he'd envisaged himself saying, 'but you'll have to move into the master bedroom. And you're never to cover that beautiful body of yours with clothes.'

A quite irrational fury fuelled his tongue.

'Aren't you aware that your father no longer owns this house?' he snapped. 'You have no right to be here. No right at all.' *And no right to make me want to seduce you!*

'Look, I can explain,' she said in a lilting voice which was as attractive as her singing, 'but it's rather difficult talking through the door.'

'Then come out and explain,' Russell commanded gruffly.

'I can't. I don't have any clothes with me. And I'm not coming out wrapped in a towel!'

Russell grimaced. Little did she know but he'd seen her in a lot less.

It was no wonder he hadn't recognised her, he supposed. He'd never seen Power's daughter in the flesh before, so to speak, only a few times on the TV news, hosting one of her never-ending birthday parties. Her twenty-first a few years ago had been so obscenely expensive that it had received extensive coverage. Admittedly, she hadn't been on the TV lately. He did recall seeing her on the news about six months ago, going to the première of a movie, sashaying up the red carpet, dressed up to the nines and with not a hair out of place as she'd flashed her pearly whites for photographers.

He'd always thought her the ultimate rich bitch, groomed within an inch of her life. He'd also cynically believed that nothing about her skin-deep beauty was real, especially her long blonde hair. He'd imagined she was a product of a good plastic surgeon and an expert hairdresser.

Now he knew that she was a natural beauty and a natural blonde, courtesy of that small triangle of fair curls he'd glimpsed between her legs.

Damn! He had to stop thinking about things like that.

'What say I meet you downstairs in ten minutes' time?' she suggested through the door.

A sensible suggestion, but it irritated him all the same. This whole scenario irritated him.

'Make it five,' he countered sharply, before whirling on his heel and heading for the door.

CHAPTER FOUR

NICOLE gritted her teeth, any embarrassment she'd been suffering from swiftly replaced by annoyance. She might not have any right to be here, but he had no right to be rude, whoever he was. There certainly wasn't any need to treat her like some criminal, not once he'd discovered who she was.

Nicole wished she'd insisted on knowing who *he* was.

A security guard perhaps?

He'd *sounded* like a security guard. He certainly hadn't been a gentleman.

When a peek into her bedroom showed that he'd left, Nicole set about finding something to wear. Not the wrap-around skirt and top she'd worn on the plane. Or any of the crushed clothes in her backpack.

She would have to select something from the wardrobe she'd left behind.

There was a lot to choose from in the walk-in wardrobe. Nicole shook her head when she saw that some of the items still had their price tags on them. All of them carried designer labels too, and most of them were on the glamorous side. Not the kind of thing she wore these days.

Jeans would have to do, she decided. Jeans and a simple black T-shirt.

Both were designer pieces but at least they didn't look it!

The five-minute limit she'd been given was fast approaching by the time she found some clean underwear and got herself dressed. She would have to hurry, since it was imperative she not antagonise the man waiting for her downstairs. The last thing she needed was for him to demand she leave without giving her the opportunity to do what she'd flown back to Sydney to do.

As Nicole quickly wound her damp hair up into a loose knot on top of her head, she regretted not having packed up everything she wanted the moment she'd arrived this morning. That way, she'd have been long gone by now. Unfortunately, when her flight had touched down at Mascot at six this morning, she'd been totally wrecked. She hadn't slept a wink all night because of a crying baby in the seat behind her. So when she'd let herself into the deserted house—which didn't even have a For Sale sign outside of it—sleep had beckoned. She'd stripped off and dived straight into the bed which had been hers since the age of nine. It hadn't occurred to her that anyone might come and find her here.

Now she was in the awkward position of having to ask the grump downstairs for a favour. Her name—which had once opened doors to her—was not going to be an asset, either. The name of Power was probably mud around Sydney these days.

With a sigh, Nicole slipped her bare feet into a pair of black mules and made her way reluctantly to the door.

She heard him before she saw him, marching back

and forth across the marble-floored foyer, his heavy footsteps echoing through the house. As Nicole crossed the carpeted landing which led to the curving staircase, she began picturing an overweight fellow in his fifties with a power complex. So the sight of a tall, dark-haired, well-built man in his mid-to-late thirties came as a surprise, as did the clothes he was wearing.

Nicole might have reached the stage when an expensive wardrobe had lost its appeal for her, but she still recognised top-quality clothes when she saw them. This man's navy-blue suit was definitely not off-the-peg. Aside from the faint sheen on the material, which shouted a mohair blend, the single-breasted jacket was superbly tailored, with not a wrinkle where the sleeves met the presumably padded shoulders.

For surely they couldn't be his *real* shoulders, Nicole thought a touch cynically as she started walking down the stairs. Men who wore suits like that were rarely renowned for their physical fitness.

David had looked extremely well built in all of his business suits. But he'd not been quite so impressive once he'd undressed.

Nicole grimaced. She was always doing that nowadays, finding things to criticise about her ex-fiancé. Yet once she'd thought him fantastic. More fool her!

Suddenly, the man downstairs stopped that infernal pacing and glanced up.

For the first time during the last four months, Nicole was grateful for something her stepfather had once given her—a modelling and deportment course which had also concentrated on self-control and discipline.

She'd never needed both of those things more than at the moment when this man's eyes met hers.

Blue, they were. Not a bright or a brilliant blue, but an icy blue, about the same colour as his shirt.

It wasn't the colour of his eyes which rattled her, however, but the intense dislike she glimpsed in their chilly depths.

For a split second her step faltered, but then she continued on down the stairs, smiling at him and pretending he wasn't looking at her as if she was his worst enemy.

All the while she was wondering why he was so antagonistic towards her, as well as who he might be.

She'd presumed, when she'd first seen his expensive business suit, that he'd been sent from the bank that had repossessed the house. Now that she could see him better, however, she changed her mind on that score.

He didn't look like a banker. His thick, wavy black hair was worn too long for that career, just reaching his collar at the back. There was also something decidedly unconservative about his roughly hewn features. If she wasn't mistaken his nose had been broken at some stage. And there was the hint of a five-o'clock shadow around his strongly squared jaw line.

Put him in less elegant clothes, and one would have thought he did something physical for a living. Physical and dangerous.

A prize fighter, maybe. Or a pirate.

'Sorry to keep you waiting,' she apologised politely as she reached the bottom step.

Russell almost laughed. She wasn't sorry about anything.

Females like her thought the world was their oyster. Of course, being rich *and* beautiful was a powerful combination. Though possibly, now that her doting father's financial situation had changed, she would have to rely more on her beauty.

It irked Russell that he found her just as attractive with her clothes on, though that image of her in the nude wasn't far from his mind. It also irked him that she looked fantastic without any of the artifices that were rich bitches' stock-in-trade.

Not a single scrap of make-up adorned her lovely face, not to mention her even more lovely green eyes.

Hadn't he known they'd be beautiful?

Of course, they were her mother's eyes.

He stared hard at her and tried to see what she'd inherited from her father, beside her natural air of self-containment.

'And you are?' she asked coolly as she stretched out her right hand towards him.

'McClain,' he ground out, steeling himself as he shook her hand. Touching her in any way, shape or form could be hazardous, so he kept any contact as brief as possible. 'Russell McClain.'

'That name rings a bell,' she said, a delicate frown creasing her forehead. 'Have we met before?'

'No.'

'I didn't think so,' she mused aloud. 'But...' The frown abruptly disappeared, replaced by a smile which twisted Russell's gut into a terrible knot. 'I know who you are now,' she said with a flash of recognition. 'You're the McClain on all those For Sale signs around Sydney. You're McClain Real Estate.'

'That's me,' he admitted.

'So you've been hired to sell the house.'

'No.'

She looked taken aback. 'I don't understand. If you're not here as a real-estate agent, then why are you here?'

'I'm here, Ms Power,' he said, his mouth curving in anticipation of his moment of triumph, 'not to sell this house, but to take possession of it. As of an hour ago, it's mine, along with all its contents.'

Once again, he was denied satisfaction. Because she didn't look devastated. Just surprised.

'Goodness! That was quick. Did you get a bargain?'

'I paid the market price,' he said somewhat stiffly. Why wasn't she more upset?

The answer was obvious: because she already knew about the bank's repossession and probable fire-sale. Why? Because she was still in touch with her doting father.

'Mmm,' she said. 'I would have thought the bank might have auctioned it. But no matter. My only concern is removing my personal things.'

'Why didn't you remove them before this?' he asked abruptly.

'I would have if I'd known the situation. But I didn't. I've been overseas for the last few months. Although once Mum contacted me and told me what had happened, I flew back straight away. My plane got in first thing this morning. I honestly didn't think it would cause any trouble if I came here to collect my things. I didn't mean to stay long, but I was so wrecked after the flight that I couldn't resist a sleep.'

'I see,' he bit out. Now he knew why she hadn't been in the news lately. She'd been overseas. Probably staying in various playgrounds of the rich and famous: St Moritz, the French Riviera, maybe the Greek islands? Her skin had that warm, honey colour which indicated a life of leisure in the sun.

'Look, it won't take me too long to pack what I want,' she went on hurriedly. 'I promise I won't take anything I shouldn't. The household silver is safe, I can assure you,' she finished with another of those gut-twisting smiles.

Damn it all, what was it about this creature which entranced him so?

He wanted to hate her, but he was finding it darned difficult.

Russell vowed to try harder.

'You obviously still have a set of house keys,' he pointed out sharply.

'I promise to leave them behind. We could arrange a hiding place.'

'I don't think so, Ms Power. I'll stay till you go. That way you can hand them to me personally.'

Her shrug showed the first trace of irritation. 'If you insist.'

'I insist.'

'It could take me quite a while,' she said. 'I'll have to contact a girlfriend and get her to bring over her car. I have a lot of clothes and only a couple of suitcases.'

'That's all right. I'll wait.'

Her very pretty mouth tightened. 'You're being ridiculous, do you know that?'

'I'm being careful.'

'I only want what is rightfully mine.'

'So do I. I've paid twenty million dollars for the privilege.'

'Twenty million! Wow! And there I was thinking you were a greedy opportunist.'

Russell drew himself up to his full six feet three inches.

'I don't take advantage of other people's misfortunes,' he said, stung by her remark.

'In that case you should appreciate my situation more,' she said. 'And be a little more accommodating. I mean, you're not moving in here right this second, are you?'

'No.'

'Then what's your problem?' she threw at him, green eyes flashing. 'Surely you don't think I'm going to strip the place bare.'

'I have no idea what you might do, Ms Power. I don't know you.'

Her hands found her hips. 'Then why do you dislike me so much?'

'I don't,' he lied.

'Huh! I can always tell when someone doesn't like me, and you don't like me, Mr McClain.'

'You're imagining things,' he said.

'If I am, then goodness knows how you got to be such a success at your job. I always thought real-estate salesmen were experts in charm. You seem to have left yours at the front door.'

Russell's smile was wry. 'Aah, but I'm not trying to sell you anything, Ms Power.'

'Oh for pity's sake, call me Nicole.'

'If you insist.'

'I insist.' Her hands fell from her hips as an exasperated sigh escaped her lips. 'Look, I appreciate you must have had a shock, finding someone in your new house, especially not knowing who I was. After all, you didn't know it was me, did you?'

'No,' he replied, his mind once again going back to the sight of her in that shower. His body began recalling that sight, too.

Russell cleared his throat and did up his suit jacket. 'I thought you were a squatter,' he admitted.

'And once you found out I wasn't?'

'What do you mean?'

'You still weren't happy. When I came downstairs you glared at me like I was some kind of vermin.'

That's because I wanted you, naked again, and under me. For hours on end.

I still do.

The discomfort of his ongoing arousal made Russell brutally aware that to stay in her provocative company any longer than necessary was masochistic in the extreme. He had to get out of here, and soon.

'Now you really are imagining things,' he said. 'But you're right,' he added with one of those warm, winning smiles he reserved for his female clients. 'I am being rather ridiculous about this. So please…take your time packing your things, and stay another night, if you need to. You can drop the keys in at the Bondi branch of McClain Real Estate any time tomorrow.'

She seemed stunned by his sudden turnaround.

Russell took her speechless moment as his cue to depart.

'Goodbye, Ms Power,' he said with a small nod of his head. 'It's been a pleasure meeting you.'

CHAPTER FIVE

'I STILL don't know what it was that I said or did which changed his mind,' Nicole told Kara as they carried yet another load of clothes down to Kara's car.

It was eleven o'clock the next morning, Nicole having taken up Russell McClain's offer to stay another night.

'He went from being hostile to helpful in one second flat,' she went on. 'And then he called meeting me a pleasure! I tell you, I've never been so bamboozled in all my life.'

Kara gave her a knowing look. 'You fancied him, didn't you?'

'You have to be joking! He was the rudest man I've ever met.'

'Yep,' Kara said, totally unruffled by her best friend's denial. 'You fancied him.'

Nicole sighed. 'I shouldn't have.' But Kara was right. Underneath the natural antagonism she felt at the way he'd treated her, she *had* fancied him.

Maybe she had a secret yen for the dark and dangerous type. Or for men with cold eyes and a personality to match.

But now Nicole realised that she hadn't been fooled by his switch from chilly to charming, just confused.

'Was he very good-looking?' Kara asked as they trudged upstairs again for the umpteenth time.

'You wouldn't have thought so,' she told her petite and slightly plump friend, who always went for the pretty-boy type. 'Too tall and too macho for you.'

'What did you say his name was?'

'Russell McClain. Of McClain Real Estate fame.'

'Never heard of him. But you know me—I have absolutely no interest in business.'

An understatement. Kara's family were old money and high society. Kara didn't have to work, so she didn't. Nicole could now see that her best friend's charity-luncheon, party-going lifestyle was extremely shallow, as hers had once been. But she still loved Kara, who had a kind heart and would never deliberately hurt anyone.

Unlike other people with money...

'This McClain guy has obviously done very well for himself,' Kara said. 'You did say he paid twenty million for this place, didn't you?'

'That's right.'

'You should have been nicer to him.'

'I *was* nice to him,' Nicole protested. 'Till he made it perfectly clear that he didn't like me for whatever weird and wonderful reason. Oh, what am I doing, taking all these clothes with me?' she said once they reached the walk-in wardrobe again. 'I know I said I wasn't going to leave a single thing behind for that man to throw away, but this is insane. It's not as though I would wear most of them any more. Especially these,' she said as she scooped up an armful of evening gowns.

'I can't understand why not,' Kara said, taking the last few dresses down from the racks. 'They're all utterly gorgeous. I think you've gone a bit far with this new social conscience of yours, Nickie darling. You don't have to dress like a tramp to do good in this world. And you don't have to sell all your lovely jewellery, which arrived first thing this morning, by the way. You must know you won't get even half what it's worth. What you need,' she went on as the girls made their way downstairs again, 'is a seriously rich husband who'll give you an unlimited credit card, then leave you alone to do whatever you like with his money.'

'While he does whatever *he* likes,' Nicole pointed out archly. 'The last man on earth I would ever marry is a seriously rich man.'

'Megan is.'

Nicole stopped just inside the front door to throw her friend a puzzled glance. 'Megan who?'

'Megan Donnelly. Surely you remember her. She was in the class below ours at school.'

Kara and Nicole had attended a private girls' boarding-school which only the very well-heeled could afford.

'I can't put a face to the name,' Nicole said, frowning.

'She was a pretty brunette with big brown eyes. But terribly shy.'

'Oh, yes, I remember her now. She was a good artist, wasn't she? Used to do all the school posters.'

'That's the one.'

'Who's she marrying?'

'James Logan.'

Nicole's eyebrows arched in surprise. James Logan was the high-profile owner of Images, Sydney's biggest advertising and management agency. She'd met him socially a few times, and, whilst he was extremely good-looking with a highly polished persona, there was something about him which she didn't like.

'He's been married before, hasn't he?' she said on their way down to the front steps. 'To that model, Jackie something-or-other. Golly, I'm bad with names.'

'Jackie Foster. Yes, they were divorced a couple of years back. He must have given her a huge settlement because she doesn't work as a model any more. Rumour has it she bought a house in Acapulco and is living there with her new partner. Women like her are never alone for long,' Kara finished up with a flash of uncharacteristic cynicism.

'Or men like him,' Nicole replied just as drily.

'True.'

'I wonder what he sees in Megan,' Nicole said as she laid the evening gowns on top of the huge pile on the back seat.

'Who knows?' Kara replied with an airy shrug. 'But he isn't called the makeover man for nothing. I imagine it will be a very different Megan who swans down the aisle on Saturday afternoon. I can't wait to see what she looks like. That's everything, isn't it?' she said, and slammed the hatchback door shut.

'I should hope so. How come you got an invitation to Megan's wedding, by the way?' Nicole asked. 'I mean, it's not as though you and she were close friends.'

'Her mum and my mum play bridge together. Would you like to come? I know for a fact that there have been a couple of last minute drop-outs, which annoyed the bride's mother no end. I could easily get you an invite. It's black-tie, but that won't be a problem for you, not with your wardrobe.'

'I don't think so, Kara.'

'Don't be silly. My whole family's going. You'll still be staying at our place on Saturday, won't you?'

Nicole didn't want to impose on Kara's parents, or stay in Sydney any longer than necessary. But it would take time to sell her jewellery, if she wanted a fair price.

Thinking of selling her jewellery gave her another idea. Why not sell off most of her totally useless wardrobe as well? There was an up-market second-hand shop in Double Bay that bought designer clothes and accessories, especially items which hadn't been worn, or worn hardly at all. Nicole's mother had been a regular customer over the years, having developed the snobbish and almost obscene habit of not wearing any outfit more than twice.

'Well?' Kara piped up. 'Does that face mean a yes or a no?'

'It's a yes,' Nicole said. 'If you're sure your mum doesn't mind.' When she'd rung Kara this morning, it had worried her that Kara's family might not want to have anything further to do with her, now that she was the daughter of a runaway bankrupt who'd clearly left a lot of angry people behind.

'Will you stop being so silly? Of course Mum won't mind. She thinks you're terrific. That settles it, then. You're coming with us to Megan's wedding. If nothing else, you'll get a good feed, which you look like you need. And who knows? You might meet some gorgeous guy who'll sweep you off your feet and keep you in Sydney for a while. I've really missed you, you know, sweetie. Life hasn't been the same without your *joie de vivre*.'

Nicole pulled a face. 'I lost my *joie de vivre* back in June.'

'Then it's high time you found it again. At Megan's wedding.'

'I'm not sure I'm in the mood for a wedding. But I'll go, provided you do me one favour.'

'What's that?'

'After we lock up here, I want you drive to the Bondi branch of McClain Real Estate.'

'What for?'

'I've been ordered to drop off my set of house keys there. But I don't want to go in myself. Would you do it for me? I don't want to run the risk of seeing that man ever again!'

'Coward,' Kara said with a cheeky grin…

'You needn't have worried,' Kara told her half an hour later. 'He wasn't there. He's out playing golf. But the receptionist said she'd been instructed to text him as soon as the keys arrived.'

'And did she?'

'Oh, yes. Straight away.'

'I can imagine. The man's a natural bully. Was there any message back?'

'I didn't wait to find out.'

'Oh…'

'For a girl who didn't want to see him again, you seem very interested in his movements.'

'I just don't want him getting back to me about anything.'

'How can he, when he doesn't have a clue where you're staying in Sydney? You didn't give him my name or address, did you?'

'No.'

'Then you don't have to worry. The odds of your running into Mr Bully McClain again in a city of over four million people are next to zero!'

* * *

Russell read the text message without any visible reaction. But he had to make a conscious effort to relax his stomach muscles as he and Hugh walked to the next tee.

He'd been enjoying their golf game so far, finding it a pleasant distraction from thinking about the day before and his frustrating run-in with Nicole Power. He was also one shot in front, which was rare. Although a naturally talented sportsman, Russell didn't play enough to seriously challenge Hugh, who spent more time on a golf course than he did behind his desk.

Russell wished now that he hadn't asked Barbara to text him when those wretched keys arrived. All it had done was bring back disturbing memories—and even more disturbing desires.

Still, he'd been wise to get out of that house when he had yesterday. Even so, he'd had a dreadfully restless night, his male hormones giving him hell. Now they were back on high alert again.

Under the circumstances, he might be forced to pick up some starry-eyed female at James's wedding this weekend. He couldn't see himself lasting too many more nights without having some extremely satisfying sex.

Meanwhile, he had a golf game to win.

'You do realise Jimmy-boy doesn't love Megan,' Hugh said just as Russell lined up for his drive on the tenth hole. 'He's only marrying her because she's pregnant.'

Russell stopped his backswing in time, shooting Hugh a exasperated glance. 'Are you trying to put me off? Because if you are, you've chosen the wrong tack. I already know all that.'

Russell should have anticipated Hugh's disapproval. The three of them had been mates since school and knew each other very well. Of the trio, Hugh was by far the softest and most romantic in nature, despite having garnered a well-deserved reputation over the last decade as one of Sydney's most notorious playboys.

'He actually admitted it, did he?' Hugh said, indignation in his voice.

'No. He didn't have to. Look, Hugh, we both know James is still hung up on Jackie. He's marrying Megan to get what she couldn't give him: a family.'

Russell had no problem with that. Sometimes, a man had to do what a man had to do.

'He *is* overseas on business, isn't he?' Hugh asked with a scowl on his face. 'He's not still seeing that wretched woman, I hope.'

Hugh had not liked Jackie. He'd thought her a gold-digger. Hugh claimed to be able to spot members of that species at first sight, his position as only son and heir to the Parkinson Media fortune making him an expert on the subject.

'Not that I know of,' Russell said. But he wouldn't put it past his friend. Since his divorce, James had developed a ruthless streak which surpassed even his.

James's courtship of Megan had been a classic example. He'd pursued the girl with a passion which had even fooled Russell for a while. But soon after their engagement had been announced six short weeks ago— the day after Megan told him she was pregnant—James had done a flit overseas, minus his adoring and unsuspecting fiancée. He wasn't due to return till tomorrow, the day before his wedding.

Russell suspected that the pregnancy had been planned. Not by Megan, but by James. No way would he want to find himself with another wife who couldn't have children, which had been the unfortunate case with

Jackie. When she'd discovered that she was infertile Jackie had insisted on a divorce, refusing James's suggestion that they try IVF or adoption. Russell had never seen his friend so distraught as he'd been at that time in his life.

Not that James had openly voiced his distress. He was not a man to talk about his personal problems. Neither would he ever let them totally rule or ruin his life.

Hence his marriage to Megan, who was one of the sweetest girls Russell had ever met.

'It's all right for you,' Hugh said somewhat disgruntedly. 'You're not the best man. You don't have to make a speech. How can I stand up there and rave on about how much James loves Megan when I know it's not true?'

'Could we leave this conversation till I've hit off?' Russell replied, then promptly smashed the golf ball a good sixty metres down the fairway, at least twenty metres past Hugh's ball.

Hugh whistled. 'What's got into you today? You suffering from a testosterone overload or something?'

'Possibly,' Russell replied, his mind once again filling with the image of a certain blonde standing naked in that made-for-two shower. 'You might as well know, I guess. Yesterday, I bought Alistair Power's mansion in Belleview Hill.'

Hugh wasn't surprised, which was understandable. Both Hugh and James knew how he felt about Power. The three of them had been room-mates at uni when Russell's father had committed suicide. He'd confessed everything that had happened afterwards to the other two. Although they'd never discussed it, they'd known what had been driving Russell all these years.

'For how much?' Hugh asked.

'Twenty mil.'

'But you'd have paid double that, wouldn't you?'

'Yep.'

Hugh cocked his head on one side, his expression speculative. 'Just how much were you responsible for what happened to Power Mortgages?'

'Power's greed was ultimately responsible,' Russell bit out. 'I just gave things a helping hand.'

'I can imagine,' Hugh muttered. 'So is that it, Russ? Is it over?'

Russell shrugged. 'There's nothing much more I can do, is there? Power's escaped. And I doubt very much if he's broke. He's probably out there on some island in the Bahamas, sipping pina coladas.'

'Let it go, mate. Let it go and move on.'

'That's easier said than done. Getting even with that bastard has become a way of life.'

'I do see that. But like you said, you've done all that can be done. It's time you made a different life for yourself.'

'And what, exactly, would you suggest?'

'You could consider having a real relationship with a girl for a change? Perhaps even consider a child or two?'

Russell stared at his friend. 'Am I hearing you right? You're suggesting that I do what James is doing? Marry some nice girl I don't love just to have children?'

'Who says you won't love her? From what I've seen, you've never given love a chance. You might surprise yourself.'

'I *never* surprise myself. I'm just like you, my friend. I don't do love and commitment. But enough of me. Back to your problem as best man. Why don't you rave on about how much Megan loves James?' Russell sug-

gested as he swept up his tee, then shoved his jumbo-
sized driver back in his golf bag. 'That's true enough.
Then concentrate on how beautiful a bride she is. No
one will notice that you don't mention the bridegroom's
affections. Leave it up to him to lie. He's obviously
very good at it.'

'I don't get it,' Hugh grumbled as they made their
way down the fairway. 'I would have thought you'd
have seriously disapproved of this marriage. You're
always going on about honesty being the best policy.'

'There's honesty and honesty, Hugh,' Russell replied.
'Sometimes a little white lie doesn't do any harm. James
will make a good husband and father. Megan will never
know that his heart is elsewhere.'

'Don't be too sure about that. Some day, someone is
going to say something. Jim should have told her the
truth from the start. She would still have married him.'

'I doubt that. A girl as sensitive as Megan wouldn't
like being short-changed in the love department.'

Hugh sighed. 'Marriage is a trap for all players, especially when big money's involved. I don't want
anything to do with it.'

'You've certainly made no secret of that.'

'One has to learn from experience,' Hugh pontifi-
cated. 'And from history. I'm just like my father. I need
variety when it comes to women. My boredom thresh-
old is spectacularly low. What I don't need, however, is
a string of ex-wives, like dear old Dad has acquired.
He's damned lucky that none except my mother
produced offspring, or he'd be broke by now.'

Russell laughed. 'Broke? The man's a billionaire ten
times over!'

'That's beside the point. For an intelligent man, Dad

is extremely thick about his sex addiction. I've learned the difference between love and lust, and I live accordingly.'

'Give the man a medal.'

Hush's bedroom-blue eyes shot daggers at Russell. 'You can be a judgemental bastard, do you know that?'

'Yes.'

'Hypocritical as well. You criticise my sex life yet you're doing pretty much the same.'

'We're both bad bastards when it comes to the fairer sex.'

'Not as bad as Jimmy-boy. I have a dreadful feeling about this marriage, Russ. Do you think it's too late to talk him out of it?'

'I've already tried.'

'And?'

'You know James. He's as stubborn as a mule. Now, let's stop this futile conversation and play golf.'

Hugh shrugged resignedly. Russ was right. Jim was not good at taking advice. But it was a shame, he thought. Megan was a darling. Not his type, of course. He liked women with spirit.

Thinking of women with spirit reminded him of the one woman in his life who had too much spirit—his PA, Kathryn.

What a slave-driver! She actually expected him to go to the office every day, and made her disapproval loud and clear when he didn't. Lately he'd found himself actually going to work most mornings, just to shut her up. It was no wonder Russ was beating him today. Hell, he hadn't played golf in over a week!

The situation could not continue. He'd have to get rid of her. But how? She'd never given him any cause to fire her. She was perfection as an employee. Capable and conscientious, never taking a day off, never arriving late or leaving early.

Her fiancé had his pity. She was going to make a dreadful wife. A real nag, keeping tabs on him every minute of the day and always wanting everything to be just so.

Of course, there would be some compensation for a husband putting up with her unrelenting standards. She was, without doubt, one of the sexiest women he'd ever met.

Not pretty, or beautiful.

Sexy.

'You've just walked right past your ball,' Russell pointed out.

'What? Oh, yeah…right.'

'I can see now why I'm winning. Your mind is elsewhere. So what's the problem? A woman?'

'Got it in one.'

'Can't get her into bed, is that it?'

A light went on in Hugh's brain. He hadn't realised up till this moment why he'd hired Kathryn Hart in the first place, and why he was now thinking about firing her.

'You've hit the nail right on the head, Russ,' he muttered. Damn, why hadn't he realised this earlier?

'You'll find a way, mate,' his friend said drily. 'You always do.'

CHAPTER SIX

NICOLE'S gasp of shock sent Kara's head whipping round to face her friend.

'What is it? What's wrong?'

'It's him,' was all Nicole could manage.

'Who?' Kara frowned as she followed the direction of Nicole's stunned gaze to the three men who stood at the head of the church aisle. 'You can't mean the groom. And you certainly can't mean the best man. That's Hugh Parkinson. Everyone in Sydney knows Hugh Parkinson. So you must mean the groomsman. I don't recognise him.'

'You said the odds of my running into him again were zero,' Nicole muttered under her breath.

'*That's* Russell McClain of McClain Real Estate?'

'The one and only.' Looking sinfully sexy in a sleek black dinner suit.

'He's better-looking than I thought he'd be.'

'He's had a haircut and he's wearing a tux. All men look good in tuxes.'

'No, not all men. Though Leyton does, don't you, darling?' Kara said, hooking arms with the man by her side.

Leyton was Kara's latest in a long line of boyfriends.

Kara was inclined to be on the fickle side and Nicole didn't even try to keep up with the passing parade of pretty boys her friend had dated over the years.

'Don't I what?' Leyton replied a little vacantly.

Intelligence was not something Kara valued in a man, unlike Nicole, who could not abide stupidity.

'Never mind,' Kara said, patting Leyton's hand.

The bride's arrival put paid to any further conversation over the amazing coincidence of Russell McClain being at this wedding. Though it wasn't till the bride started walking down the aisle that Nicole managed to drag her attention back to the present.

Megan still looked like Megan, Nicole thought as the bride moved past her pew. There'd been no radical makeover. Though she did look truly lovely in a strapless ivory dress which had a tightly boned and heavily beaded bodice and a huge gathered skirt. Under the long veil—which was held in place by a simple coronet of tiny roses—her dark brown hair was tightly pulled back from her beautifully made-up face, an exquisite pearl necklace adorning her slender neck.

'Doesn't she look fabulous?' Kara gushed.

'Absolutely gorgeous,' Nicole concurred.

Unfortunately, once the bride had passed by, Nicole's mind returned to the third man at the head of the aisle. Why, oh, why, did fate have to be this cruel?

Fortunately, he wasn't looking down into the congregation, so he hadn't seen *her.* Still, it was just a matter of time.

Nicole shuddered at the thought of meeting him again.

The ceremony was simple and very traditional. It was also quite short and soon the wedding party moved off into the vestry, presumably to sign the register. It wouldn't be long before they'd be walking back down the aisle, right past where Nicole was sitting.

'Just going outside for some fresh air,' Nicole said. 'It's very stuffy in here.' Before Kara could stop her she jumped up and slipped out the back, heading straight for the oak tree in the corner of the churchyard.

It was the perfect hiding place, the tree's large trunk keeping her out of sight whilst its huge canopy of leaves provided shade from what was an unseasonably hot day for early November. Although it was getting on for five in the afternoon, it was still extremely warm and surprisingly humid for this time of year. A storm was predicted for later in the evening but not soon enough to spoil the wedding. At the moment, there wasn't even a cloud in the clear blue sky.

A sudden burst of noise and laughter indicated that the ceremony was over, a glance around the trunk confirming that the wedding party had emerged from the church, followed by waves of guests, most of them armed with digital cameras and photo-taking phones.

Nicole stayed hidden whilst all the photographs were taken, but not so hidden that she couldn't get a few surreptitious glimpses of the annoying man whom she didn't want to fancy…but did.

Finally the wedding party left, and Nicole called out to Kara, who was obviously looking for her.

'So there you are!' Kara said. 'What are you doing, skulking off in this corner? As if I don't know! Come on, we're off to the reception. And before you say it, no, we can't possibly take you home. It's too far for one thing. Leyton would have to drive back across the harbour bridge, then back again. The reception is being held at a yacht club not far from here.'

'I could always take a taxi,' Nicole said. She was no longer stone-broke, having sold a good proportion of her wardrobe yesterday.

'Mum would not be pleased if you did a flit. And the mother of the bride would be livid. You're stuck, sweetie. Not that I'm sure why you'd want to run away. Your Mr McClain is quite yummy, if you like the gladiatorial type. And he's not into the second brides-maid, by the way, even though she practically glued herself to his side during the photographs.'

'How do you know that?' Nicole had been feeling quite jealous of the attractive redhead, whose burgundy satin bridesmaid dress had showed an impressive cleavage.

'Because he hasn't even *looked* at her boobs,' Kara said. 'And just about every other man has, I can tell you.'

'He can look if he wants to,' Nicole said offhandedly. 'What do I care?'

'Oh, come, now, Nickie. You don't fool me for a minute. You've got the hots for the guy.'

'I wouldn't go that far.'

'I would. You know, I don't understand what your problem is. In the old days, you'd have just sashayed up to him and in no time flat he'd have been toast.'

'That was then and this is now,' Nicole said, thinking that what Kara said was true. She used to have great success in attracting the opposite sex, and great confidence.

But David had destroyed a lot of her self-esteem, his critical words still stinging.

'The trouble with girls like you,' he'd thrown at her when she returned his ring, 'is that you think being drop-dead gorgeous is enough for a man. But it isn't. What we want is a woman with some passion in her veins, not some vain little puss who expects to just lie back and let the man do all the work.

'And that's another thing,' he'd added. 'If you think I'm sorry this engagement is over then you can think again. You might be beautiful to look at, sweetheart, but you're a bloody bore in bed.'

Ever since that day, whenever a man had looked at her with interest Nicole had run a mile.

A light suddenly went on in her brain. Up till now, she'd convinced herself she'd seen nothing in Russell McClain's eyes the other day but dislike.

But now she realised that was not strictly true. Along with the dislike, she'd glimpsed something else.

Desire.

Unfortunately, this time, Nicole didn't want to run a mile. Despite her fear of further humiliation, she *wanted* to sashay up to him at the wedding reception. She *wanted* him to be toast.

But she just didn't have the courage, or the confidence.

Kara sighed a long, exasperated-sounding sigh. 'Whatever am I going to do with you? That creep has a lot to answer for.'

Nicole blinked up at her. 'What creep?'

'David, of course. Who did you think I meant? Surely not Mr McClain. He hardly qualifies as a creep. He was nice to you in the end, wasn't he?'

'I suppose so.'

'You worry too much these days. Come on, let's go. Leyton's already gone back to his car and he'll be wondering where we are.'

Nicole reluctantly allowed herself to be led away, all the while thinking she should never have agreed to come to this wedding in the first place. At the same time she could not deny that there was a small sliver of excitement running through her veins at the prospect of meeting Russell McClain again.

At least she was looking her best, having been to the hairdresser's first thing this morning with Kara, then having spent quite a long time afterwards on her body. Months of not bothering had been reversed as she'd buffed herself to the max. Her make-up had taken her almost an hour, but overall the final result had been most pleasing.

The dress she was wearing—one of only a few dresses she'd not sold yesterday—was a pale green, empire-line, halter-necked number with a low-cut draped bodice and a swishy skirt which finished just above her knee. More of a party dress than the kind of thing one wore to a snooty wedding. But she'd always liked it.

She hadn't been going to wear jewellery, despite having not sold any yet. But Kara had talked her into donning the emerald and diamond set Alistair had presented her with on her twenty-first, which consisted of a pendant and two drop earrings.

'This is a society wedding, sweetie,' Kara had said somewhat impatiently. 'If you're not going to wear a more formal dress, then you have to at least wear some serious bling, not to mention decent shoes.'

The handmade Italian shoes Kara had produced for her to wear were extremely glamorous, a slender crisscross of exquisitely beaded straps somehow managing to anchor her feet to their very high heels. Stockings had been out of the question, so Nicole had sprayed her legs with some fake tan to match the natural tan she had acquired on her upper half in Thailand.

'No sitting in a corner tonight,' Kara said during the

drive to the yacht club. 'I want to see you up and dancing and having some fun.'

'In these shoes?'

'Shoes never stopped you in the past. And if a certain someone asks you to dance then you must promise me you won't say no.'

'You can be terribly bossy, do you know that?'

'*I* do,' Leyton interjected—though not unhappily.

'Promise?' Kara insisted.

Nicole didn't have to promise any such thing. Because if Russell McClain asked her to dance, she knew she would not be able to say no. All she could hope was that he wouldn't ask her.

Because there was something about the man which she didn't trust—and she'd had enough of untrustworthy men.

'OK,' she said. 'I promise.'

CHAPTER SEVEN

RUSSELL'S frustrated gaze was scanning the guest tables in search of feminine prey when his eyes landed on the very female who'd put him in this appalling state in the first place.

His heart lurched at the sight of her. So did something else.

Blast! What on earth was Nicole Power doing at James's wedding?

His gaze shifted to the rest of the people at her table, but he didn't recognise any of them. There again, he didn't recognise most of the guests. Despite his wealth, he wasn't a social animal. Not like James, or Hugh; they enjoyed entertaining and being entertained. Russell had had had other priorities up till now.

His need for revenge had consumed him.

Now something else was consuming him.

The more he stared at her, sitting there looking absolutely delicious in the sexiest green dress, the more he wanted her.

Had she seen him yet? he wondered.

She must have. He was in the main wedding party. Strange that he hadn't spotted her before this. Perhaps she was deliberately avoiding him? He could well understand why: he'd been pretty obnoxious the other day.

Hugh suddenly leant over from the chair next to him.

'I see you're eyeing that hot-looking blonde over there,' he said. 'Presumably, you haven't recognised her. That's Nicole Power, your enemy's daughter.'

'Yes, I know.'

'You *know*?'

'Indeed I do.'

Hugh frowned. 'Russ, you're not going to take this revenge of yours too far, are you? I mean, she's not to blame for what her father did.'

Up till this moment, Russell hadn't thought of his attraction for Nicole Power as anything more than extremely annoying. The thought of using his unexpected and, up till now, unwanted passion as a weapon against his enemy had never occurred to him.

But, suddenly, the vengeful words he'd thrown at Alistair Power all those years ago took on an added meaning: he'd vowed to take everything his enemy held dear…

Clearly, Power held his daughter dear…

It *was* a wickedly tempting idea…

'What do you know about her?' Russell asked Hugh abruptly.

'If you think I'm going to help you seduce that poor girl, then you have another think coming.'

'She's far from being poor, Hugh. I'll warrant those are real diamonds and emeralds she's wearing. And that dress has designer label written all over it. She might not be personally responsible for what her father did, but she's never minded living off the proceeds.'

'You don't know that.'

'Yeah, Hugh, I do. Now, tell me what you know about her.'

Hugh sighed. 'She was briefly engaged to David Porter earlier this year.'

'The stockbroker?'

'Yep.'

'What happened? Wasn't he rich enough?'

Hugh shrugged, clearly not happy with giving him any information at all. 'I have no idea. Porter's not in my immediate social circle. But I've heard he's a ladies' man. Maybe she found out she wasn't going to be his one and only.'

'I doubt that.' Russell could not conceive of any man being unfaithful to Nicole Power. If she were *his*, he wouldn't let her out of his sight...he'd keep her chained to his bed.

'When does the dancing begin?' came his abrupt question.

'Not for a while. First come the speeches, then the cutting of the cake, followed by the bridal waltz. After which, other people can join in.'

Russell's smile was wry. 'Sounds like you've been to a lot of weddings.'

'My family and friends don't seem to learn from experience. This is the second one for James as you will recall. Dear old Dad has had four more wives since my mother.'

'Presumably I won't ever have to go to yours, then.'

'Not unless some alien takes possession of my body and forces me into it.'

'What about this woman who won't go to bed with you? You might be reduced to marrying her, just to get her in the sack.'

Hugh looked appalled. 'Marry just for sex? You have to be joking. No man's that desperate these days.'

Russell's eyes went back to the object of his own desire.

He was a man and he wanted Nicole Power, quite desperately.

But Hugh was right. You didn't marry a girl just for sex. But what about revenge? Did you marry a girl for that?

His conscience rebelled at the idea. But his dark side didn't. It revelled in the thought of having his cake and eating it, too.

His eyes narrowed as they raked over the sheer perfection of her face, which was even more beautiful today. Of course, she was wearing make-up and her upswept hairdo had obviously been done by a professional. All in all, she was the epitome of feminine beauty: a fair-haired siren with a breathtaking allure which would tempt any man.

Russell was more than tempted.

His head whirled with wildly tantalising thoughts. How would it feel to possess her, body and soul? To have her look at him, not with irritation as she had the other day, but with passion? Maybe even love?

Would that satisfy his vengeful soul, having Nicole Power fall in love with him?

Russell suspected that it might.

Such thinking, however, was a fantasy at this moment. If he wanted to know how it felt, he'd have to make his fantasy come true.

Somehow.

His lips pursed as his mind began to plan.

She was obviously unattached at the moment, having been seated with women on either side of her at the table.

But being unattached was not enough.

He wasn't as handsome as James, or Hugh. He was a country boy, a bit of a rough diamond, so neither did he possess his friends' natural charm.

What he did have, however, was money. Lots of it.

As much as he believed Alistair Power was still supporting his daughter, he knew that girls like Nicole Power could never be too rich. It was also a point in Russell's favour that he wanted her to the extent that he did.

Women, he'd found from experience, liked being wanted, even more than they liked being loved. They were often seduced by the flattery of being pursued, of being the object of uncontrollable desire.

I wanted you from the first moment I saw you, were very seductive words. He'd used them to great effect before.

This time, they wouldn't be a pick-up line, either. They'd be true. With a bit of luck, he might be able to sweep Nicole Power off her feet and into his bed with those passionately delivered words, after which he hoped to obtain her total sexual surrender via his skills in the bedroom.

Russell didn't pretend to rival Hugh's Casanova-like reputation but he knew how to make love. He genuinely liked female bodies, liked touching them, kissing them. He liked their softness and sweetness, their curves and their cavities.

Once he'd got a girl into his bed, she rarely wanted to leave. The trick with Nicole Power would be getting her into his bed in the first place.

Russell was staring at her and planning his course of action when her head suddenly lifted and their eyes clashed.

She didn't look away immediately. She held his gaze for several startled seconds before turning her head and engaging the curvy brunette next to her in conversation.

'I suggest you give her a miss, mate,' Hugh said. 'Why not try Kristy? She's as keen as mustard.'

Russell grimaced at the mention of the bridesmaid who'd been his partner for the marriage ceremony. 'A little too keen for me,' he replied drily.

'In that case you won't mind if I—er—'

'Feel free.'

'Great. Oh, oh. Toast and speech time. Mine, unfortunately. By the way, I did what you suggested and concentrated on Megan's love for James. Hope she doesn't notice that anything's missing.'

'She won't. She's obviously besotted.'

Russell glanced along the curved table at the bride, and then at James, who'd been doing his best imitation of an equally besotted bridegroom all day. At their small and very select stag party last night—just drinks for the three of them at the Belleview Hill house—Hugh had refrained from asking James too many questions about his trip overseas, perhaps not wanting to know the truth.

What was to be gained by discovering that James had spent some time with his ex; that he might even have slept with her?

Russell already suspected that something had happened between James and Jackie. He'd seen the bleakness in his friend's eyes last night when James had thought neither Russell nor Hugh were looking.

Hopefully James would find some happiness married to Megan, he might even fall in love with her in the end.

No, that was the sort of romantic crap Hugh came out with. James wasn't going to fall in love with Megan any more than *he'd* fall in love with Nicole Power.

Russell didn't delude himself about the ruthless individual he'd become over the years. His plan to cold-bloodedly seduce his enemy's daughter tonight was wicked enough. To even consider marrying her was truly wicked.

But that was getting ahead of himself.

She might tell him to get lost later tonight. In a way, he hoped she would. Because if she didn't, she would put him on a path from which there might be no turning back.

Frankly, to have anything to do with her was risky, even downright dangerous. He could pretend she was his prey, but for how long? *He* was the besotted one here. *She* was the one with all the potential power.

Once she knew he was attracted to her—a man with millions—then the tables could well be turned. She might set her cap at *him*.

Russell had to laugh.

'What's so funny?' Hugh asked.

'Just the perversity of life, mate.'

'Don't tell me about it. I already know. But it's not life that's the main problem. It's women.'

'You could be right there.'

'I am right, Russ. Take my word for it.'

Russell's eyes turned to again seek out the woman currently giving him problems.

But her chair was empty.

CHAPTER EIGHT

NICOLE stood at the railing of the deck which over-looked the marina. The night sky was overcast, the air still sultry with not much breeze coming off the water. In the distance, several flashes of sheet lightning heralded the storm which had been forecast for later that evening.

Nicole knew she should return to the reception, but she simply could not. To sit there and be the subject of that man's never-ending stare was beyond her.

She didn't have to look back at him after that first time to know that his eyes were constantly upon her. She could *feel* them raking over her, burning into her, making her aware of her body in ways which were as disturbing as they were embarrassing.

Her fiercely erect nipples were bad enough, especially since she wasn't wearing a bra. Even worse was the dampness between her thighs.

Nicole had stayed in the powder room for several minutes, after which she'd escaped outside, hoping that some fresh air would bring her wayward flesh under control.

But the air outside was hotter than the air inside.

She *felt* his presence before he spoke, her skin breaking into instant goose-pimples.

'We meet again, Nicole,' he said quietly as he materialised next to her.

Nicole's fingers tightened around her evening bag before lifting it from the top of the railing. Slowly she turned to face him, grateful that he could not hear her heart thudding behind her ribs.

'Did you get your keys?' she asked him with creditable cool.

His smile was light and might have been charming on any other man. But not on him and not when accompanied by the predatory gleam which glittered in his cold blue eyes.

'Indeed I did,' he said. 'I hope you got everything you wanted from the house.'

'Yes, thank you.'

'I was surprised to see you here. I presume you're a friend of Megan's.'

'We went to the same school.' No way was she going to explain her presence here any more than that. It would make her sound like some charity case.

'What are you doing out here?' he went on. 'You missed all the toasts and speeches.'

Trust him to notice. But then he would, wouldn't he? He'd been watching her all evening. And now he'd followed her out here.

Nicole could not pretend that she didn't know the reason why. She'd been the object of male pursuits ever since she'd left boarding school. Up till her experience with David, she'd enjoyed the mating game.

But that had been before she was told she was a bore in bed.

'I had a headache,' she invented.

'Have you taken something for it?'

'Yes,' she lied again.

'And?'

'I'm feeling better.'

'In that case, would you like to dance?' he said, his blue eyes fastening hard onto hers again.

Lord, but they were powerful, those eyes. And oh, so sexy.

'I...I think I'd rather stay out here,' she replied, somewhat shakily.

'That's all right. The music's loud enough. We can dance right where we are.'

Before she could find some other excuse, he took her bag, placed it on top of the railing, then drew her into his arms.

'I'm sorry if I was rude to you the other day,' he said softly as he began to move her back and forth in a slow, sensual rhythm.

Nicole swallowed, but didn't say anything in return. Her brain was far too busy trying to get a handle on the wild heat rushing through her. His holding her even more tightly did little to free her mind, or soothe her instant panic.

'I have a confession to make,' he whispered into her ear, which was now perilously close to his mouth. 'From the first moment I saw you, I wanted you.'

Nicole jerked back out of his arms, her eyes widening as they flashed up to his.

'I dare say you've had many men say that to you over the years,' he went on. 'Please believe me when I say I don't make a habit of such rash declarations. That's why I was rude to you at first, because the intensity of my feelings took me by surprise. And because I was sure that a girl as exquisitely beautiful as you are would already be taken. But your being here tonight, alone, indicates that maybe I was mistaken…' His eyebrows lifted questioningly. 'Is there a lover or boyfriend in your life at the moment? Someone overseas perhaps?'

Nicole still couldn't find her tongue, but she did manage to shake her head in the negative.

The satisfaction in his eyes was both flattering and frightening. 'Then I'm free to tell you that seeing you again tonight has done nothing to lessen my interest. In fact I want you more than I've wanted any woman before in my life.'

The passion in his voice, and in his eyes, both dazzled and dazed her.

'You take my breath away,' he ground out, cupping her chin firmly with his right hand and lifting her mouth up towards his rapidly descending lips.

His kiss was not gentle. But she loved it, wallowing in the bruising force of his lips and the savage invasion of his tongue.

If he'd stopped within a decent span of time, she might have had some common sense left. But he went on and on, draining her of the rest of her will, pushing her beyond any thought of where this would end, beyond everything but the need to keep on being kissed by him.

His wrenching his lips from hers brought a soft cry of dismay.

Russell stared down at her parted lips and dilated eyes and wondered if this was all for real—for *him*, Russell McClain, the man.

Her surrender seemed amazingly quick, as though she was possessed by the same mad passion which had governed both his lust-filled words earlier and his kisses just now. But it didn't seem logical that the coolly composed creature he'd met the other day would suddenly turn into a wanton.

Of course, party girls like her did live a pretty fast life. For all he knew, she could be on something tonight, some recreational drug which had lessened her inhibitions and heightened her appetite. Or maybe she'd imbibed too much of the top champagne James had had flown in from France for his wedding; a few glasses of that could make a girl very amenable to a man's advances.

On the other hand, maybe she'd had some time to think about her changed circumstances since arriving back in Sydney. Maybe she'd decided that Daddy's lessened wealth might not last forever and she would need a new gravy train if she wanted to continue the good life.

Which meant this show might not be for him, Russell McClain, the man...but for Russell McClain, the potential billionaire.

Perversely, Russell no longer cared what her motivation was for looking up at him as if she couldn't wait to go to bed with him. All he cared about right at that moment was where she would be before this night was out. He'd never felt anything like the arousal he was feeling right now. His flesh had moved beyond pleasure and into the realms of sheer and utter pain.

'So there you are!'

Russell suppressed a groan at the arrival of the plump brunette Nicole had been sitting next to inside.

'I was wondering where you'd got to,' the girl added, her eyes avid as they flitted from one to the other. 'Have I interrupted something, sweetie?' she directed at

Nicole. 'If so, please just say so and I'll go. I'm nothing if not discreet.'

Nicole blushed furiously, surprising Russell. It was hard to fake a blush. There again, it could be a blush of guilt.

'Nicole and I are just leaving,' he stated firmly.

The brunette seemed startled but not displeased.

'Would you mind, Kara?' Nicole said, still looking faintly embarrassed.

'Of course not. Off you go and have some fun. I'll leave a key to the back door in the usual spot. But I won't fret if you don't use it. If your bed's still empty in the morning, I'll tell Mother you've gone out on a breakfast date with a handsome hunk you met at the wedding. Nice to finally meet you, Mr McClain.'

She flashed him a saucy little smile, making him wonder what Nicole had said about him to her.

Obviously something.

'*Au revoir*, sweetie,' she finished up and, with a flamboyant wave, whirled around her plump but not unattractive frame to head back to the reception.

By this time, Russell and Nicole weren't alone on the deck, several more people having made their way outside.

'Come on,' Russell said, sliding a captive arm around her waist and guiding her along the deck towards a set of steps which would take them down to the car park.

'Where…where are we going?' she asked breathlessly as he hurried her towards his car.

'Not to a club, that's for sure.' Or to his apartment, despite it being the closer of his two current residences. He'd moved a few things into the Belleview Hill mansion yesterday and slept in Alistair Power's king-sized bed for the first time last night. Once again, however, the experience had lacked the feeling of satisfaction he'd been anticipating.

Russell could see, however, that sleeping there tonight with his enemy's daughter by his side would be a whole different ball game. Now, *that* would feel like real revenge, of the highly personal kind that he'd always coveted.

He zapped the car unlocked, reefed open the passenger door and had her inside in record time.

'This is crazy,' she said after he'd climbed in behind the wheel. 'We hardly know each other.' And she shot him an oddly fearful look which didn't compute with her being drunk, or drugged, or directed by materialistic ambition.

She seemed genuinely alarmed at her own behaviour, which was as puzzling as it was a possible problem. Russell didn't want her having second thoughts at this stage.

He shoved the key in the ignition, then leant over the gear stick to take her face in his hands once more.

'What is there to know but this?' he murmured, and kissed her again. Softly this time and seductively, savouring the low moan of surrender she made when her lips flowered open under his.

Now that he had her where he wanted her, Russell wasn't about to let her get away. He pressed her hard against the leather seat and kept on kissing her, at the same time letting his right hand slide slowly down her neck till it reached the valley between her breasts.

Once there, he quite deliberately lifted his mouth away so that he could watch her eyes when his hand moved underneath her dress and over her naked breast. He wanted to see her reaction, wanted to watch for signs of anything fake.

Not that it really mattered. If she was pretending desire for the sake of greed, then the outcome would not change: he would still bed her tonight.

But having Nicole Power mindless with desire for him would be an added bonus. How ironic would that be? How brilliantly satisfying!

His hand moved and her eyes flung wide open, her back stiffening when his fingers found their goal.

Her nipple was hard, like a river pebble.

'No, don't,' she whimpered when he rolled it round and round with his fingertips.

He ignored her feeble protest and kept doing it till her mouth gasped open and her eyes glazed over. At that point he pushed the silky green material aside to totally expose her breast, then bent his head to put his mouth where his fingertips had been.

Her practically jackknifing from the seat told Russell all he needed to know. There was absolutely no pretence in her responses. She was his, to do with as he pleased. His to explore and exploit. His to win and maybe even to wed.

Did he want to go that far? Did he want to see her walk down the aisle in white the way Megan had that day? Did he want to see blind adoration in her eyes as well as the mindless desire he'd just glimpsed in her beautiful green eyes?

There was only one answer to those questions.

An unequivocal yes.

CHAPTER NINE

NICOLE squeezed her eyes tightly shut against the sensations bombarding her body.

Oh, yes, she thought wildly when he sucked harder on her nipple. *Yes!*

Her hands closed into tightly balled fists by the sides of the seat, her bag having long slipped out of her grasp. She pressed her back against the leather and lifted her chest higher for him, inviting his mouth to take in more of her breast.

His sudden desertion dragged a groan from deep in her throat, her eyelashes fluttering open to stare up into the darkly silhouetted face looming over her.

'As much as I'd like to ravage you right here and now,' he said thickly, 'I think it best that we wait till I get you home.'

A stunned Nicole just sat there as he returned to the driver's seat and started up the engine, several seconds passing before she realised her left breast was totally exposed, its peaked nipple still glistening with his saliva.

'Leave it like that,' he growled when her hand moved to cover herself up.

'I...I can't,' she said, shocked by the suggestion.

'Someone might see me.' And she quickly pulled her dress back into place.

'As you wish, beautiful,' he said as he sped off.

As I wish?

Nicole's eyes darted across to the man behind the wheel, her gaze landing on his hands first. Big they were, and strong.

What she wished was that they were on her body again. His mouth, too, on her breasts and between her legs.

Nicole shuddered at how thrilling she found that thought. How thrilling she found him, wickedly thrilling.

Oh, yes, he was wicked all right.

But oh, so passionate. The things he'd said to her back at the yacht club, the things he'd done to her just now in this car…

She was still thinking about those things when his car zoomed down into the harbour tunnel and she realised where he was taking her: to her old home in Belleview Hill. But now it had become his, for twenty million dollars…

This last thought brought her back to some semblance of sense, reminding Nicole of her recent vow never to have anything to do with rich men. Not only were a lot of them corrupt and amoral, but most were also arrogant and spoiled and far too used to getting their own way.

Russell McClain was undoubtedly all of those things. Just look at the company he kept! Hugh Parkinson was a roué, if ever there was one. As for James Logan… Nicole hoped Megan would be happy with him, but she doubted it.

So what on earth was she doing going home with him?

Nicole had never been a one-night-stand kind of girl. In the past, she'd thought of herself as a prize for the man who was pursuing her, a prize worth waiting for. She'd been taught by her once-bitten mother to put tickets on herself in that regard, to not give herself cheaply and easily.

Which she hadn't.

She'd dated David for two months before they'd slept together.

Still, David had never made her crave him the way she was craving Russell McClain right at this moment. She could not stop thinking about it, could not wait to feel again what this man could make her feel.

His being rich was irrelevant at this moment. No doubt she would regret her impulsive behaviour in the morning. But future regrets had no chance of making her do or say anything to stop the man sitting next to her from having his wicked way with her tonight.

By the time Russell arrived at his destination, the demands of his cruelly frustrated body threatened to override his need to control this situation, himself, and her.

Nicole's silence during the drive had given him far too much time to think about the rest of the evening, his desire for her body, plus the anticipation of finally getting even with Alistair Power through his daughter, proving an intoxicating mix. He could not wait to take her, to watch her come apart in his arms.

But that would only happen if he could control his own excruciating need for release.

Not an ideal situation.

But still his priority remained to whip her up to Power's master bedroom, where the greatest revenge of all could begin.

'You don't have a girlfriend tucked away somewhere,

do you?' Nicole suddenly asked as he drove through the gates. 'Or a wife?'

Russell's eyebrows lifted. Hardly the question a totally turned-on girl would ask.

But typical of women like Nicole Powers. They always had their eyes on the ball.

'Of course not,' he said truthfully.

'You…you wouldn't lie to me, would you?'

Something in her voice pricked his conscience.

'Why would I do that?' he answered a little gruffly.

'To get me into bed.'

He parked at the base of the front steps and turned off the engine before facing her. 'I've never had any trouble getting women into my bed before, Nicole. And I haven't had to lie.'

He reached out and touched her flushed cheek before trailing his fingers over to her mouth. Slowly, he traced her lips with a single fingertip till her mouth fell open on a low moan. He might have inserted his finger for her to suck if he hadn't already been on a dangerous edge himself.

'There's no need for me to lie to you,' Russell lied as he let his hand drop away. 'You're an adult woman, Nicole. You've come here with me willingly, so let's not play games with each other. Let's just enjoy tonight for what it is. A man and a woman totally in tune with each other. Come on, let's get out of here and go somewhere a lot more comfortable.'

She didn't protest when he took her hand and led her up the curving staircase into the master bedroom. But she did look a little shell-shocked, her eyes widening when they landed on the bed, which he'd fortunately had the foresight to make that morning, complete with its French lace duvet.

'You can't expect me to sleep with you in my mother's bed,' she choked out, her bag clutched defensively in front of her.

'*My* bed now,' he said, removing that infernal bag and tossing it onto the bedside table before pulling her into his arms again. She went, but rather reluctantly, which was not what he wanted. He wanted her mindless, as she'd been back in his car.

'Come, now, Nicole, you're…how old?'

'Twenty-five.'

'Old enough not to worry about such things, then. Your mother is a woman of the world. Do you really think she'd care?' he finished as his head began to descend.

No, Nicole realised just before he kissed her. She probably wouldn't. All her mother cared about these days was the good life. It didn't even bother her that her husband was unfaithful.

But still…being in her bed didn't feel right.

Any qualms she had about where Russell made love to her, however, were obliterated within seconds of his lips meeting hers, that incredible craving returning with an urgency which brooked no excuses or objections. Soon, all she cared about was that his mouth was back on hers again. His hands, too.

A small degree of panic resurfaced when he stopped kissing her long enough to turn back the duvet. She whispered a feeble protest when Russell started undressing her, but he just said, 'Don't be silly,' and kept on stripping her till she was totally naked, except for her jewellery.

His stepping back and just staring at her at that stage brought a rush of dark excitement, the like of which she'd never known before. Although not in any way ashamed of her body, Nicole had never been an exhibitionist. Having Russell's hungry eyes raking over her bare skin, however, sent her head spinning, her nipples peaking under his hot gaze, her belly tightening with the most delicious tension.

'Take the jewellery off,' he commanded in a desire-thickened voice.

She managed to unhook the drop earrings and put them on the bedside table, but fumbled with the clasp of the pendant.

'I'll do it,' he ground out, and strode round behind her.

She shivered when his fingers grazed the nape of her neck.

'Was this a present?' he asked as he slid the released necklace from around her throat.

'Yes,' she choked out.

'From a besotted admirer, no doubt. No, don't bother to answer that. I haven't brought you here to discuss your past conquests,' he said as he dropped the necklace next to the earrings then turned her round to face him.

'Frankly, I prefer you without adornment of any kind,' he said, his eyes narrowing as they travelled slowly over her totally exposed body.

Nicole didn't know what to say or do. So she just stood there and let him look at her, her mouth bone-dry, her heart racing behind her ribs.

He didn't make any move to touch her, just continued to stare at her till the air in the room grew a lot warmer and her head a lot lighter. When she swayed, he caught her by her shoulders, spun her round then yanked her hard against him. Once there, he released her shoulders and snaked his left arm tightly around her waist, holding her solidly captive while his other hand was left free to do as it pleased.

And it finally pleased to touch her, his widely splayed palm rubbing back and forth over her fiercely erect nipples till she didn't think she could bear any more.

'Oh, please,' she whimpered.

A flash of lightning accompanied by a huge clap of thunder brought a different cry to her lips.

That tantalising hand stopped abruptly, the room suddenly very quiet except for his heavy breathing. Nicole stiffened when another loud clap of thunder rocked the room.

'You're frightened of storms?' he asked, his mouth hot against her ear.

'Yes,' she choked out.

'I love them.'

'What's there to love about them?'

'They usually herald rain. Farmers' sons love rain.'

When his hold on her suddenly slackened, Nicole wriggled round in his arms and looked up into his flushed face.

'You're a farmer's son?' How did you become one of the most successful real-estate agents in Sydney? she thought.

'Once upon a time,' he said wryly, his eyes growing distant as they turned away to glance around the room. When they eventually returned to hers, his face had cooled, his expression no longer that of a man in the throes of passion.

Yet when he smiled, a strangely erotic shiver trickled down her spine.

'Enough of this chit-chat,' he said, and abruptly scooped her up into his arms. 'Time to get down to business.'

CHAPTER TEN

RUSSELL scooped her up into his arms and laid her down in the middle of the bed, kissing her with cold deliberation before withdrawing to stand at the side of the bed.

That storm had arrived just in the nick of time, reminding him of why he'd brought Alistair Power's daughter here in the first place. Not just to satisfy his lust—which he was certainly aiming to do—but also for a far more satisfying goal.

Revenge.

Which was better taken slowly and with a cool head.

For several seconds he just stared down at her, drinking in her exquisitely beautiful body, which was even more tempting than he remembered. She looked delicious spread out like that with her legs slightly apart and her hands laid on the pillows beside her head.

The sudden thought that he would prefer her tied to the bed startled Russell. He'd never been partial to that kind of thing before. But the image of her spread-eagled and bound and totally helpless almost brought his resolve to be cool and controlled totally undone.

He had to pull himself together, had to find some composure or all would be lost. There would be no triumph for him if he became her prey. *She* was the prey here. She was the instrument of revenge, even if she didn't know it.

Clenching his teeth hard in his jaw, he willed his wayward flesh to behave, then slowly, very slowly, began taking off his clothes, not dropping them on the floor but draping each item neatly over a nearby chair: jacket, tie, shirt and belt.

Once he was naked to the waist he extracted his wallet from his trouser pocket, took out two condoms and put them on the bedside chest. After that he took off his shoes and socks, placing them tidily under the chair before unzipping his trousers and removing them with all the speed of a snail.

He was playing for time, of course. Time to give his painfully swollen flesh the chance to subside a little.

He wasn't all that successful. The sight of Nicole's near-naked body was way too arousing. So was the thought that, soon, she would be his.

Another flash of lightning came, along with a clap of thunder even louder than the last. The storm was getting close. So was the storm which was about to break in this room, a storm which had been years in the building.

Nicole shivered, both at the sound of the thunder and the sight of Russell's almost naked body. He was magnificently built. Tall and broad-shouldered, with a flat stomach and an enviable tan, making her wonder how he had acquired the latter. Not from a gym, that was for sure. Maybe he surfed, or swam outdoors.

He had a smattering of dark curls between his well-defined chest muscles. His legs were long, with nicely shaped calves and powerful thighs.

She could not help but compare him with David,

who'd been extremely handsome, facially, but not so impressive without his clothes on. He'd had no shoulders to speak of, plus pale skin and a flabby belly.

Russell's abruptly dropping his boxer shorts had Nicole swallowing hard. Oh! Now he very definitely left David in the shade.

Thinking about David, however, brought a jab of panic which found voice when Russell joined her on the bed.

'I…I should warn you about something,' she blurted out.

His face immediately darkened. 'There's nothing you can tell me that I want to hear. Not right now, anyway.'

Russell took a few moments to don protection, after which he rolled back and kissed her. Then kissed her some more.

A big mistake.

But he could not seem to stop, especially when she wound her arms tightly around him, one of her hands finding the back of his head and pressing his mouth down on hers even harder. The sounds she made deep in her throat were as exciting as they were distracting, heating his blood and turning his head to mush. Desire dictated his actions as his hand slipped down between her legs, her gasps of pleasure bringing him dangerously close to the edge. There was nothing cold-blooded in his actions when he spread her by then trembling thighs and surged into her. Revenge was far from his mind as her hot flesh closed tightly around him, his mouth bursting from hers with a raw groan, his heart going like a jack-hammer in his chest.

Her eyes met his, wide with excitement and something else.

Wonder shone up at him; a wonder that was as surprising as it was achingly sweet.

She looked as if she'd never felt anything like what she was feeling at this moment.

A minute or two ago, Russell would have experienced triumph.

Now he just wanted to keep that wondrous look on her face.

It was a struggle to control his own desperately swollen flesh, but he managed, wrapping her legs around his waist before rocking back and forth inside her with a gentle rhythm, finding immense satisfaction, not by indulging in vengeful thoughts, but in seeing the extent of her pleasure. She didn't have to say a word, her body speaking for her, her mouth dropping open, her face flushing wildly, her head twisting from side to side.

When her eyes closed tightly shut on a strangled cry and her internal muscles stiffened around him, Russell realised he could let himself go. Immediately he scooped his hands under her buttocks and lifted her up hard against him, his heart thundering in his chest as he surged more powerfully into her.

Her eyes flew back open as she climaxed, her gasping sounds still full of that highly seductive wonder, as though this was a first-off experience for her. Russell empathised with how she felt when he found release and it was much more intense than he could ever remember. Consumed with the sudden need to hold her closer, he lifted her up off the bed and pressed her body to his. When her arms wrapped tightly around his neck and her head dropped to his chest with a shaky sigh, he could have stayed like that forever.

But, as his excitement faded, Russell came back to earth with a thud. This was Nicole Power he was getting all sentimental over, the rich-bitch daughter of Alistair

Power, the man he'd vowed to destroy. She wasn't some innocent little flower having her first sexual experience. She was a well-known party girl who'd probably had more lovers than designer dresses. The odds of sleeping with him being a super-special, uniquely pleasurable experience were remote. He was good in bed, but he wasn't *that* good.

More likely she'd decided to act the *ingénue* with him tonight, thinking that might appeal to his possibly jaded sexual appetite. Hadn't he concluded earlier tonight that she might be on the look-out for a rich husband?

For pity's sake, get real, Russell, my boy, he warned himself. You didn't bring your enemy's daughter here to lose your head over her much practised charms.

It was fortuitous that she chose that moment to lift those gorgeous green eyes of hers, her expression unbelievably bewildered.

'That was amazing,' she said with soft awe in her voice. 'Truly amazing.'

Yeah, right, he thought cynically. And I'm the king of England.

Russell almost laughed. Still, it had been a close call there for a while. There'd been a point when he'd almost surrendered to her spell, when all thought of revenge had been banished from his mind.

That was what was truly amazing.

He'd have to watch himself with her. She was different from any female he'd ever been with before. She made him *feel* things.

Russell came to a swift decision. One night of vengeful sex would have to do, his earlier fantasy of wooing his enemy's daughter—with a view to marriage—simply too great a risk. Come morning, he would take Nicole Power back to her friend's place and never see her again.

Meanwhile, however, he aimed to see just how far she was prepared to go to catch herself a wealthy husband.

But, first, a trip to the bathroom was called for.

'Be back in a sec, sweetheart,' he said before pulling away abruptly and heading for the *en suite* bathroom.

CHAPTER ELEVEN

IT TOOK a few seconds for the penny to drop. *Nicole* might have thought what had just happened was truly amazing. But Russell didn't agree, if the look on his face and the speed of his departure were anything to go by.

In hindsight, Nicole could see that she'd acted more like a virgin bride than the woman of the world Russell must have thought he was taking to bed. Not only had she run true to form by letting the man do everything again, but she'd also gone all gooey afterwards.

The thought that Russell might be in that bathroom, wondering why he'd wanted her so much, brought a groan of dismay. It was patently obvious, now that her brain was re-engaged, that sex with her hadn't lived up to his expectations.

Nicole groaned a second time. Why hadn't she insisted he take her in the car?

She'd wanted him to.

Nicole vowed then and there that when Russell emerged from that bathroom, she would be a lot more adventurous and assertive. She would not wait to be touched or kissed. *She'd* do the touching and kissing first.

She was lying there, working up the courage to put

her thoughts into action, when a flash of lightning lit up the huge balcony outside the master bedroom. Almost immediately, there was the most deafening crack of thunder and Nicole felt the bed under her actually shake.

And then all the lights went out.

Nicole didn't scream, which was an achievement of the highest order.

But she was clutching the sheet up around her throat when she heard the bathroom door open.

'You all right?' Russell called out to her through the darkness.

'Yes,' she managed to answer without sounding too much like a frightened rabbit.

'I'll see if it's just us that's blacked out,' he continued matter-of-factly, 'or the whole neighbourhood.'

More flashes of lightning gave Nicole a good view of Russell as he crossed the room, heading for the French windows which opened onto the balcony. He was still naked, she noted, with the sexiest butt she'd ever seen.

Nicole found herself hoping that all of Sydney was blacked out. Then Russell wouldn't be able to do anything but come back to bed.

'Bloody hell,' he swore after he'd opened one of the windows, then swiftly pulled it shut again. 'It's frigging freezing out there.'

'Come back to bed, then,' she heard herself suggesting with some of that boldness which she'd vowed to embrace. 'I'll warm you up in no time.' Goodness! Had that sounded too slutty?

'I'm sure you could,' he said with a wry little laugh. 'And trust me, I'll take you up on that promise in about ten seconds. But first, I need to know the extent of this blackout.'

This time, when he opened the door, Nicole heard rain, great heavy drops, hitting various surfaces. The lightning had retreated for the moment, leaving the balcony—and the bedroom—in complete darkness.

'Well, it's not just this house,' he informed her on re-entering a short time later. 'The whole local area is blacked out. But the lights over in the city are still on. It's the same with the bridge and the north shore. Which means at least James's wedding night won't be spoiled. And that reminds me…'

When he lifted the duvet and dived in next to her, Nicole stiffened. It was a last-minute attack of nerves, not a response to his chilled skin, but she decided to pretend the latter was the case.

'Oh, you poor darling,' she murmured as she forced herself to snuggle up to his side. But she struggled to keep her hand from trembling as it landed in the middle of his chest before beginning a somewhat tentative journey downwards. 'You *are* cold.'

'Not for long, I'll warrant,' he returned in a voice which, in the pitch black, sounded strangely edgy.

Her heart leapt when her fingers grazed the tip of his manhood. So did Russell's, if the abrupt expansion in his chest was anything to go by.

Nicole took a deep breath. This was alien territory to her. She'd never deliberately caressed any man like this before. Or—heaven forbid—taken one into her mouth. She couldn't imagine liking the taste or the experience.

The thought sent a weird little shudder down her spine. Not a shudder of outright revulsion, more a shudder of fear that she might make a total hash of it.

For, surely, Russell would have had scores of experienced partners who knew exactly how to perform to perfection.

Nicole's nervous swallow was swiftly followed by an irritated purse of her lips. Don't be such a coward, she lectured herself. Just do the best you can. Think of him as an ice cream, one of those choc-tops you used to buy at the movies and which you always tried to make last as long as you could.

When her hand encircled him, his groan startled her, her head jerking up to stare at where she imagined his face was.

'You don't want me to do this?' she choked out.

'You know I do,' he growled back.

She hadn't known any such thing.

The reassurance of his words, however, gave her a decided buzz. And the courage to continue.

Levering herself up into the darkness, Nicole leant over him.

Once again, he groaned. This time, though, Nicole recognised the sound for what it was.

Excitement.

She felt his flesh swell even further.

His being turned-on turned her on. Suddenly, what she was about to do no longer smacked of desperation but of desire. She actually *wanted* to make love to him with her mouth.

Amazing!

Russell braced himself for the first contact of her lips. But it was no use. He simply had no weapons against the feelings which had begun rampaging through him the moment she touched him.

He bit back another groan as her mouth encircled

him, making his back arch up from the bed and his body break out into a sweat.

She stopped immediately, but she didn't say anything or let him go. The room became deathly silent except for his own heavy breathing, a good twenty seconds ticking away before the sheer power of his need forced him to speak.

'Don't stop,' he said in a voice that contained more plea than order.

He almost cried out with relief when she actually took him all the way into her mouth.

There was certainly nothing of the *ingénue* act any more, any illusion of innocence obliterated by the expertise she was now demonstrating. Russell began wondering how many other men she'd enslaved in this way.

Was she playing him like a fish?

Either way, Russell, my boy, you should be lying back and enjoying her well-practised skills, not gnashing your teeth and working yourself up into an emotional lather over her past. That is Nicole Power down there, the daughter of your enemy. What better revenge than to have her service you in this subjugated fashion?

He should not have been worried. He should have been triumphant. But as his swollen flesh teetered on the brink of release, Russell could not get past the thought that he was in danger of becoming the victim here, not her. This would be *his* humiliation, not hers.

But, oh…the sensations she was evoking were intoxicatingly seductive. All he had to do was surrender and the most mind-blowing climax would be his. He was close now. Achingly, agonisingly close, his eyes squeezing tightly shut as his flesh strained towards release. He felt her lips tighten around him.

It was no use, he accepted with a raw cry and gave up his struggle for control.

Surprisingly, Russell experienced no sense of humiliation, only ecstasy, followed by the most blissful peace.

'That was amazing,' he heard himself say afterwards, echoing what she'd said to him earlier.

More amazing was the strange wave of tenderness which washed through him when his hand drifted down to play with her hair.

'No, don't move,' he said. His body was totally spent, his mind was already close to shutting down, and sleep was beckoning.

'Beautiful,' he murmured just before the curtain came down.

CHAPTER TWELVE

NICOLE didn't realise for a while that Russell had fallen asleep. Her brain was somewhat befuddled by what had just happened. Talk about a mind-blowing experience!

She still could not believe how much she'd loved doing it to him like that. Did that happen to other girls? Or only besotted ones?

Which she obviously was. Besotted, bewitched and, yes, somewhat bewildered.

Even now that he was asleep, the temptation to wake him again was strong. She could do it, her being with Russell having tapped into a side of herself which had obviously been dormant before. She'd suddenly discovered what it was to be a woman in the most primal sense. But to rouse him from sleep to satisfy her own surprisingly fierce need would be a totally selfish act.

He was obviously exhausted.

Not so herself. She was more awake and more alive than she'd ever been in her life.

Nicole decided that the best course of action would be to get out of this bed and away from temptation.

Very slowly and very carefully she left him, the bed and the room.

Her destination was the kitchen, where all the candles were kept. Given the speed of her mother's departure from this house, Nicole didn't think she would have taken such incidentals with her. From the looks of it, the only things she'd taken were clothes and jewellery.

The candles were sure to be there in the kitchen cupboard, along with matches. At least that would give them some light. Who knew how long this blackout would last? From the sound of the wind and rain outside, Sydney was being lashed by quite a storm.

Unfortunately, all the lightning seemed to have stopped and there wasn't a hint of moonlight. Everything was pitch-black as Nicole inched her way down the stairs, shivering a little from the drop in temperature. With no electricity, the air-conditioning wasn't working and the air was becoming fresh, even inside the well-insulated walls.

Thankfully the candles were still where Nicole remembered, one half-burnt white candle already in a candlestick with a box of matches next to it. This she lit, using the light from its rather meagre flame to search the rest of the kitchen cupboards for more candlesticks. In the end she selected a three-pronged candelabra from her mother's huge range of silverware, inserted three unused candles from a box of six and lit them before blowing the original candle out.

She didn't head back upstairs straight away, however, curious now over just how much her mother had left behind.

When Nicole had stayed in the house the other night, she hadn't looked in all the kitchen cupboards. Once she discovered that the pantry had been emptied of food, and the fridge contained nothing but ice cubes, she'd ordered in a pizza that night, then had had Kara take her down to a local café for breakfast in the morning.

Everything was still there, she soon discovered. All her mother's very expensive dinnerware, all the crockery and cutlery and glassware. Really, when you took into account the contents of this house, Russell might have actually got a bargain!

Not that Nicole wanted any of it. She didn't.

Selecting a heavy-based whisky glass, Nicole was moving over to pour herself some water from the tap when she had a sudden thought: if Russell had moved in—which it seemed he had—maybe there was some juice in the fridge.

No, she quickly saw. But it wasn't completely empty. There were four bottles of light beer and a single opened bottle of white wine, with a silver stopper in it.

Nicole picked it up and studied the label. It was French, which meant it was probably from Alistair's wine cellar. Another bonus for Russell, she realised. Alistair's taste in wine was just as expensive as her mother's taste in furniture.

Nicole removed the stopper and took a sniff. It smelled fine. In fact, its delicious bouquet was very tempting.

What the hell? she thought, and half filled the whisky glass.

It tasted as delicious as it smelled, Nicole savouring the citrusy flavour on her tongue before swallowing. Before she knew it, the glass was empty. She almost refilled it but decided she didn't want to be drunk when she went back upstairs. She wanted no excuses for her behaviour in the morning. She wanted to look back on this incredible night with a clear memory.

Nicole returned the bottle to the fridge and rinsed the

whisky glass in the sink before picking up the candelabra and heading back the way she'd come.

It came to her, as she crossed the marble-floored
foyer and began a careful ascent up the curving staircase, that she no longer felt cold. Perhaps it was the wine
which had warmed her. Or maybe she was just growing
used to the inside temperature, which was probably
only marginally cooler than the very comfortable twenty
four degrees at which the house was usually kept.

A sudden flash of light on her left sent Nicole's head
jerking round, only to be met by a reflection of herself
in the huge gilt mirror which graced the wall halfway
up the stairs.

What an amazing sight, she thought as she stared at
her naked self in the flickering candlelight.

Often, during her partying years, Nicole would stop
at this precise spot on the staircase to check her appearance before skipping down the rest of the stairs and
making her entrance.

Nicole moved close to the mirror, frowning as she
searched her face.

Who *are* you? came the silent question. You're not
the Nicole Power who used never to go to bed with a
man till you'd known him for ages. All Russell had to
say was how much he wanted you and you were his for
the taking.

And now…now you're going back up to him for
more, aren't you?

Yet you vowed not to have anything more to do
with rich men.

You know what they are. Selfish, amoral and unbelievably arrogant. When he said he wanted you more
than any other woman, he didn't mean he wanted you

for forever. This is just a one-night stand or a dirty weekend. A *very* dirty weekend. Don't go thinking his feelings encompass anything fine or deep.

Nicole shivered as her eyes drifted down her naked body. It was the same body she'd always known, yet it was different. *He'd* changed it, changed how it responded to men, how it felt about making love.

Her flesh craved him and it would not be denied.

Nicole shook her head in defeat. There was absolutely no use trying to frighten herself off. Common sense had no sway over the power of a desire this intense. She wanted Russell to make love to her again more than she'd ever wanted anything.

Scooping in a shaky breath, she whirled and walked up the remaining stairs. Once on the landing, however, she turned away from the master bedroom to go first into what had once been her own bedroom. There, she hurried into the bathroom where she put down the candelabra and reached for the hidden pins which anchored her French roll. Having her hair up no longer fitted this bold creature who'd been born tonight in Russell's arms. It had to be worn down, she decided recklessly as she combed her outspread fingers through her hair, down and loose.

'Yes,' she whispered as it splayed out over her bare shoulders in sensual disarray. When she shook her head a couple of locks fell down towards one breast, not quite covering the nipple.

She swallowed as she stared at the starkly erect peak.

He hadn't touched her breasts since that time in the car.

But she hadn't forgotten how it had felt.

A shiver rippled down her spine at the memory.

Time to go back. Not to wake him at first. Just to

lie beside him, to feel the heat of his body, to press her skin to his.

That would be enough for now.

Russell woke to darkness, and the awareness of being alone in the bed. He knew before he felt the cold place next to him that Nicole wasn't there. He was about to leap out and go in search of her when a strange light filled the open doorway of the bedroom, pale at first, then stronger.

He saw the candelabra before he saw her.

She seemed to float into the room, the candlelight casting a golden circle over her head, like a halo. She'd taken her hair down, he noted, bringing an ethereal quality to her nudity which he found exquisitely beautiful and perversely ironic.

Because she was no angel. More like a devil, tempting him all the time to care about nothing but what she could make him feel. She was a siren of the highest order. Beautiful and bold. And, he believed, born to be bad.

As she moved closer to the bed, some light eventually fell onto his face. And into his opened eyes.

'Oh!' she gasped, and stopped abruptly. 'You're awake.'

'Yes,' he agreed coolly. 'And the electricity's obviously still not on.' Propping himself up against the pillows, he drew his knees up. He could not believe how quickly she could turn him on. She didn't have to do a thing, just stand before him in her birthday suit and he was a goner.

Nothing new about that, Russell, he reminded himself ruefully as his eyes continued to feast on her. You've been a goner since the first moment you saw her in that shower.

His teeth clenched hard in his jaw as he realised it was going to take more than one wretched night to rid himself of his lust for Nicole Power.

The sound of a cellphone ringing startled both of them.

'It's not mine,' he said, nodding towards where the sound was coming from.

'If it's Kara,' Nicole said with a groan as she put the candelabra down and picked up her bag. 'I'm going to strangle her.'

Russell welcomed the interruption. It would give him the opportunity to get himself under control.

He watched her pull out a sleek silver cellphone and flip it open. 'Hello?'

Her face immediately reflected exasperation. 'Mum! What on earth are you doing, calling me at this hour? Yes, well, it might be the middle of the day where you are, but it's the middle of the night here in Australia!'

She threw an apologetic look at Russell, who just shrugged nonchalantly. But his ears had very definitely pricked up. Maybe he would find out where his enemy had decamped to. Though who knew what he would do with the knowledge?

'Yes, yes, I know I promised to ring you when I got to Sydney but I've been very busy and…What? No, I had no trouble doing that… The house was empty… No, there wasn't a *For Sale* sign on it…' This was said with a decidedly worried glance Russell's way. 'Yes, all my clothes were still there and all my jewellery arrived safe and sound at Kara's this morning. Look, can I call you tomorrow, Mum? I was just about to go to bed…'

When Russell threw back the sheet on her side and patted the mattress, her face betrayed a flash of embarrassment. Or was it guilt?

He recalled that Nicole hadn't initially liked the thought of sleeping with him in her mother's bed. He'd had to use persuasive logic along with some passionate kisses to get her to put aside her qualms.

Now the woman herself was there, in the room with them, via a phone, reminding him again of why he was here. Not just to satisfy his needs, but also to soothe his vengeful soul.

Russell's dark side thrilled to the thought of making love to Nicole whilst she talked to her mother. Even better if she started talking to her father.

But when he patted the mattress again, she frowned and shook her head.

'I'm fine,' she said, still frowning. 'Kara's mum said I could stay at their place for a while. No, I don't need you to send me any money. I have enough. And I have a plan.'

Russell pulled a face. If he was her plan, then why wasn't she lying back down next to him? That would be the way to his wallet, and his heart. If he had one, that was.

'No, I don't want to talk to him,' Nicole went on sharply. 'It won't do any good and it certainly won't change my mind.'

She exhaled a totally exasperated sigh before slumping down on the side of the bed, her back to him.

Russell just sat there, somewhat exasperated himself. If she didn't hang up soon, he might have to take matters into his own hands.

'Don't be like that, Mum,' she continued, her tone a tad weary. 'Look, I'm too tired to argue at the moment. I really need to go to bed.'

Good idea, Russell thought, growing more frustrated by the moment.

'Yes, I know I don't usually go to sleep before

midnight, but Kara dragged me off to a wedding today and… What? Oh…Megan Donnelly, a girl we went to school with… You probably wouldn't remember her. She wasn't in our class at school but Kara's mum has become buddy-buddy with her mum and she insisted I accompany them. I couldn't really say no… Well, yes, it was rather swish… The groom was James Logan, the advertising tycoon…'

As Russell listened to Nicole answer her mother's interminable questions about the wedding, he decided he could not wait for this conversation to finish. It was time to see just who had the most power over Ms Power: her mother, or her new lover.

Russell rose onto his knees behind her and smoothed her hair back from one beautifully bare shoulder.

Nicole managed to smother the gasp which rose to her lips, her whole back stiffening as her head twisted round to glare at him.

But he wasn't looking at her. He was busy nuzzling away at her shoulder, the tantalising graze of his lips making her skin break out into goose-pimples.

'Nicole, are you there?' her mother asked.

'Yes, Mum, I'm here,' came her brusque answer.

'What did you wear, darling?'

Did she really have to answer these silly questions?

'Nothing special, Mum. Just a dress. The green one I wore on Christmas Day last year.'

'You didn't! Not to a formal wedding. Oh, Nicole, I thought I'd taught you better than that. I hope you at least wore some decent jewellery.'

Nicole had had enough of this conversation. And of Russell doing what he was doing. He *knew* she was talking to her mother. Didn't he have any sense of decorum at all? Kissing her shoulder had been bad enough. Now his hands had found their way around to her breasts.

When his wicked fingers began plucking away at her nipples, she almost dropped the phone.

'I wore my emeralds,' she choked out as she gripped the phone harder. Dear heaven, but it was hard to concentrate on anything when your head was swimming and your nipples burning.

'The ones Alistair gave you for your twenty-first?'

'Yes.'

Nicole almost cried out when Russell pulled her back onto the bed, her eyes flinging wide once she realised what he was going to do.

She clasped the phone with both hands, biting her bottom lip to stop herself from making embarrassing noises.

'Better than nothing, I suppose,' her mother was saying grudgingly. 'But you should have worn something really glamorous. You might have met someone. James Logan's wedding would have been full of suitable catches.'

She almost blurted out that she *had* met someone. But that would have started a whole lot more questions and she was desperate now to get off the phone.

'Mum, I…I really have to go. I'll call you back later this week and we'll have a nice long chat.'

'You promise?'

'I promise. Bye.'

'Bye, darling. Be good now. And if you can't be good, be careful.'

Nicole grimaced as she flipped her phone shut. These were words her mother had often used in the past when she went out on a date.

Never before had they struck home so strongly. Because she wasn't being good tonight, or particularly careful.

But, right at this moment, she didn't give a hoot.

Yes, she thought wildly as her phone slipped from her grasp. Oh, yes.

'Don't stop!' she cried out.

He didn't.

CHAPTER THIRTEEN

RUSSELL stood at the side of the bed and stared down at Nicole's naked body.

She was still dead to the world—little wonder after what he'd subjected her to. It wasn't unusual for Russell to make love to a woman several times in succession. His mainly celibate existence tended to make him needy and greedy.

But she hadn't objected. Hell, no. She'd been more than happy to accommodate him every which way. By this stage, Russell hadn't questioned if she'd been faking it. He'd been way too enamoured of her charms to question anything.

In the cold light of day, however, he rather hoped she'd been pretending. He wanted her to continue being his willing little love slave for a while longer, wanted an excuse to have more vengeful sex with her.

Because let's face it, Russell, one night simply wasn't enough to cure what's driven you all these years. You want more: more revenge, more sex. More of the very beautiful Nicole Power.

He might have joined her back in bed if he hadn't been so damned hungry. With no food in the house, there was no option but to go out and get some. The continuing blackout had put paid to a local café. Russell would have to go further afield. He knew exactly where to take her. To a place where there was electricity, plenty of food and an extremely comfy bed.

His unit at McMahon's Point.

Without hesitation, he leant down to shake her shoulder.

'There's still no electricity,' were the first words Russell said when she opened her eyes.

Nicole groaned, then closed her eyes again.

It wasn't the continuing blackout which had evoked the sound of dismay, however. More the kaleidoscope of memories which suddenly filled her mind.

She'd heard about morning-after regrets. But had never suffered from them before.

How *could* I have done the things I did last night? Nicole agonised. How could I have let him do the things *he* did?

'The water's still hot in the shower,' he continued. 'A miracle considering the time we spent in there last night.'

Nicole wished he hadn't mentioned that. What was it about this man which made her such a willing victim to his wicked demands?

She wasn't in love with him. She wasn't even sure that she *liked* him. But oh, how he could turn her on!

'Come on, sleepyhead, get up,' he ordered. 'It's after nine. I've rung the powers that be. The electricity's not expected to be on in this part of town for another couple of hours.'

Steeling herself, Nicole opened her eyes, adopted what she hoped was a woman-of-the-world expression, after which she rolled over to face her nemesis.

He wasn't naked, thank God. He was fully dressed in grey chinos and a royal-blue polo top, his darkly damp hair suggesting a recent shower. His face was freshly shaven, his chin no longer sporting the stubble which he'd used to erotic effect on her in the early hours of the morning.

He glanced up from where he'd been putting his wallet and mobile phone into various pockets.

'I don't know about you,' he said, 'but I'm famished. I can't wait till the power comes back on. Once you're dressed, we'll drive over to my apartment at McMahon's Point and I'll cook us both some breakfast.'

Nicole was totally taken aback by his offer.

His smile was wry. 'You should see the look on your face. Yes, I can cook, and no, last night was not just a one-night stand. Did you think it was?'

'It did cross my mind,' she said truthfully.

'Do you want it to be?'

Did she?

Common sense advised that it would be wise to cut and run. He was everything that she'd vowed to avoid.

The right answer was obvious. Yes, yes, let's leave it at that, shall we?

Instead, she heard herself say no. Lord, what a fool she was where he was concerned!

No...

Not a word any man usually liked hearing on a woman's lips.

But it was the right reply this time.

Russell walked round the bed and picked up her clothes from the floor. 'Try not to be too long in the bathroom,' he said as he offered them to her.

She took the clothes but didn't make a move to get out of the bed. She just clutched them to her chest.

'What's wrong?' he asked.

'I…I'd like some privacy.'

He had to laugh. 'Might I remind you that you swanned around this house naked for most of last night?'

'Yes, and look what happened.' she countered, green eyes flashing. 'I really would like to make it out of here this morning without being ravaged again.'

'Might I also remind you that you liked being ravaged?'

Her blush startled him, as did the pained expression which filled her eyes.

'Look, I…I'm not usually like that,' she said. 'Not that you'll believe me after the way I acted. You probably think I'm a total slut.' Her shoulders drooped, her eyes dropping away from his.

Russell just stood there for a few seconds, utterly speechless. If this was an act, it was Oscar-winning material. What he was seeing had to be sincere.

Which meant what?

Damned if he knew.

In the end, he sat down on the side of the bed and tried to find the right thing to say.

'So what are you usually like?' came his careful question.

When her head lifted, her eyes were shimmering with tears.

'A bore!' she blurted out.

His head jerked back. 'Come now, you can't expect me to believe that.'

'Then I suggest you talk to my ex-fiancé,' she said quite bitterly whilst dashing the tears away with furious hands. 'He informed me at length that I was the biggest bore in bed he'd ever met.'

Russell frowned. 'Is that why he broke off your engagement?'

'Lord, no! *I* broke off our engagement after I walked in on him screwing his PA on his desk. He'd have married me, bore or no. Or he would have back then, when Power Mortgages was powering along like there was no tomorrow. David wouldn't marry me now, even if I was the best lay in the world.'

'I see. You do realise he probably only said those things in retaliation. He was trying to hurt you.'

'Yes, I do see that. But he was still right. I *was* a bore in bed. I *was*,' she added, 'till I met you.'

Russell just sat there for a long moment, drinking in this quite astonishing confession. As much as his first reaction was to shake his head in disbelief, he gradually accepted that it would explain the bewilderment he'd glimpsed when they'd first made love.

When she'd said she was amazed afterwards, she might have meant it.

'I've never done *half* of the things I did with you last night,' she insisted, her expression containing some of that wonder again. 'Actually, I've never done *most* of those things.'

Russell stared into her eyes, then down at her mouth, which he'd imagined servicing many men before him.

How could he believe her? She'd been way too good at that. Way too uninhibited as well.

This had to be a line. A clever line to suck him in, the way she'd sucked him in last night. Quite literally.

When he reached out to place two fingertips against her lips, her head jerked back, her nostrils flaring wide.

'And what about that?' he asked her, watching closely for signs of lying. 'Have you done that before?'

Her eyes didn't even flicker as they held his. 'No, never.'

'Not even with your ex-fiancé?' he persisted.

'He wanted me to. But I...I wouldn't. Just the thought of it used to repulse me. That's why I was so shocked when I woke up this morning. Oh, I know you don't believe me,' she went on, distress zooming into her eyes. 'I wouldn't, either, if I were in your place.'

Russell didn't know what to make of this tack. Another clever ruse, or the truth?

Damn, but it was difficult to put aside his preconceptions about her. Extremely difficult to trust *anyone* who had anything to do with Alistair Power, especially his enemy's flesh and blood daughter.

A less emotional logic finally kicked in, reasoning that the Nicole Power he believed her to be would not be making excuses for her sexual behaviour last night. She wouldn't think there was anything wrong with it at all!

Which meant she had to be telling him the truth.

It also meant she hadn't been faking.

Russell's male pride swelled, his ego triumphant at the thought she'd been genuinely swept away by true passion. Of course, none of this meant she wasn't on the make as well. But it did mean that her desire for him was real, the same way his was for her.

This gave an added edge to Russell's sudden plan to continue their affair, not just for today but longer. Much longer. He'd fantasised about her falling in love with him. What if she did? How brilliant a revenge would that be?

'You're wrong, Nicole,' he said, cupping her face and giving her a softly seductive kiss. 'I do believe you.'

The surprised pleasure which filled her eyes produced an unexpected smidgen of guilt. But Russell quickly put it aside. None of the Powers had felt guilty about his father's suicide, he reminded himself. Not for a moment.

'I'm not saying I haven't had plenty of boyfriends,' she went on hurriedly.

'I wouldn't expect anything different,' he returned. 'A girl as lovely as you. But maybe it's time you had a boyfriend who thinks you're great in bed,' he added with a smile.

'You...you want to be my boyfriend?'

'You're not keen on the idea?'

'I was planning on going back overseas soon,' she said.

He was truly taken aback. She'd mentioned some plan to her mother over the phone. He'd thought that plan might be him. It had sounded as if she was short of money. Clearly, not so, on both counts. Daddy must still be supporting her, he realised bitterly.

The thought of her escaping overseas the way Power had, produced a rush of anger which Russell had difficulty controlling, and hiding.

But he managed. Somehow.

'Where are you going?' he asked a bit abruptly.

'Thailand. That's where I was when Mum told me to come home and collect my things.'

'Why on earth would you want to go back to Thailand at this time of the year? It's stinking hot over there.'

'You get used to it.'

'You have friends there, is that it?'

'Yes. Good friends.'

'Not a boyfriend, though.'

'No.'

'Why are you being so secretive?'

She sighed. 'I'm not deliberately being secretive. It's a rather long story.'

'One which you're going to tell me over breakfast,' he said firmly.

Their eyes clashed, hers flashing with that stubbornness he'd glimpsed the first day they'd met. 'You won't change my mind, you know.'

Whilst Russell rather admired her spirit, he wasn't about to lose her without a fight. He could be a right ruthless bastard when he wanted something. And he wanted her here, with him. He didn't want her flying off to Thailand!

'We'll see, madam,' he said determinedly as he stood up. 'We'll see. Now, in deference to your morning attack of shyness, I'll wait for you downstairs. But do try to be quick. Forget the make-up and the hair. Just put it up the way you did the first day we met. Now hop to it,' he said as he walked briskly towards the door. 'If you don't make an appearance in ten minutes, I'll be coming into that bathroom and eating *you* for breakfast!'

CHAPTER FOURTEEN

NICOLE'S first thought as she climbed into Russell's dark green Aston Martin was that it was a rich man's car.

No, a rich *playboy's* car, she amended once he'd started the powerful engine and zoomed off in the direction of the city.

No doubt his apartment at McMahon's Point would be a rich playboy's pad, with all the accessories necessary for such a leisurely existence. Nicole pictured lots of leather furniture, a Jacuzzi and home-entertainment system.

He had to be taking her there not just for breakfast but also for more fun and games.

A shiver ran down her spine at this last thought. Was she being foolish, going there with him? Clearly, besides feeding her, he was going to try to change her mind about going to Thailand.

Did she have the strength to keep saying no to his wishes? She'd already gone to mush upstairs when he'd said he believed that she'd never acted like that with any other man. When he'd offered himself as her boyfriend, she'd almost said 'yes please' straight away.

Even now, she could feel herself weakening.

She *could* put her return trip to the orphanage on hold

till the New Year, she supposed. Once she sold her jewellery, she could send Julie some money to buy Christmas presents for the kids. She didn't have to go there personally right now.

But Nicole knew if she did that, she'd probably never go. She'd get sucked into the hedonistic world which she'd turned her back on, but which was extremely seductive, especially if it meant more nights with Russell like the last one.

Nicole suppressed a groan, squeezing her eyes tightly shut as she battled temptation, plus the tidal wave of desire which just thinking about last night sent crashing through her body.

The car's sudden braking and slewing to one side snapped her eyes back open to discover a tree in the middle of the road right in front of them. Nicole grabbed the sides of her seat, but Russell managed to just miss it, grinding to a neck-whipping halt with his bumper bar against the leaves.

'That was close,' he said with an apologetic glance her way. 'Sorry if I gave you a fright. I was going too fast for the conditions.'

She exhaled a long and slightly shaky breath. 'That's all right. A miss is as good as a mile.'

'I'll take it easier from now on,' he reassured her as he backed up. 'And stick to the main roads instead of trying to find short cuts. If it was a smaller tree I'd get out and try and move the darned thing, but I haven't got a hope. Aah, there's the SES now,' he said, pointing to some men in fluorescent yellow vests coming down the road. 'They'll cut it up and get rid of it.'

'I hope so. It's very dangerous.'

A couple of minutes later they were on their way

again after being directed around the tree via the footpath.

Once Nicole's attention was back on her surroundings rather than on the man next to her, she saw evidence of last night's storm everywhere, with lots of leaves and branches on the road and pools of water at the bottom of hills where the drains had been blocked up. A few of the traffic lights were still out as well.

Finally they reached the city-centre outskirts, where the power was still on and the traffic was flowing more smoothly. Despite being early on a Sunday morning, there were lots of cars on the road.

They'd just made it onto the harbour bridge when the bag in her lap started vibrating, the ring-tone on her phone following a split second later.

'That'll be Kara,' she said as she opened the bag.

'It might be your mother again.'

'Oh, I hope not. Hello?'

'Nickie, it's me. Are you still blacked out at your place?'

'Yes.'

'Thought you might be, since we're only a few streets away. Look, Dad's started up the gas barbeque so we can have some breakfast. You and your gladiator are welcome.'

'Actually, Kara, Russell is taking me over to his apartment at McMahon's Point for breakfast. We're already on the bridge, but thanks for the offer.'

'Now, how come I'm not surprised? Must have got a clue when you didn't call this morning.' There was no sarcasm in this remark. Just mischievous pleasure.

'Sorry. How did the rest of the reception go last night?'

'Great. Megan had a gorgeous going-away outfit. I gather she and James were spending the night at a hotel in the city, then flying out somewhere romantic this morning. Couldn't find out where, it was a secret. But enough of that. How was your night? Obviously pretty good.'

No way was Nicole going to give Kara a post-mortem on her performance, or Russell's.

'The storm was bad, wasn't it?' she said instead.

Kara sighed. 'OK. I get the message. He's sitting right next to you. How about we use code like we used to when we were teenagers? Let's see, now…If he was good in bed, just say uh-huh. If he was super-good, don't say anything.'

After a few seconds' silence, Kara groaned. 'Ooh, I'm so jealous. Actually, no, I'm not at all. My Leyton's very yummy. But you haven't been too lucky in that department, have you? I mean, I've never heard you rave about a guy, not even David. So, tell me more…'

'Kara, I'm sorry, but you're breaking up. I'm losing the signal.'

'You bitch, you are not,' she said laughingly. 'That phone of yours would get reception under water. All right, I'll stop the probing. Look, before I forget, Dad has lined up a jeweller friend of his to come to the house first thing tomorrow morning to look at your jewellery. He said Max is a fair man and will make a fair offer.'

'That's great, Kara. Thank him for me, would you?'

'Will do. But you'd better come home some time tonight. Don't stay over at lover boy's place again.'

'I should be back for dinner tonight,' she told Kara.

'No, you won't,' Russell interrupted. 'You're coming out to dinner with me.'

'I heard that! He's very forceful, isn't he?'

'More like very presumptuous,' Nicole said with a reproving glance his way.

'Very smitten, I'd say,' Kara said. 'But don't let him get his own way too much. Come home after dinner.'

'I intend to, don't worry.'

'I asked Dad about him. Dad knows everything about everyone with money in this town. Anyway, McClain Real Estate has an excellent reputation for honesty and integrity. Russell McClain, however, is a bit of a mystery man. He keeps a low media profile and doesn't socialise, which is weird for someone in property sales, according to Dad. Of course, I already knew he wasn't a party-goer, or I'd have met him somewhere. Dad said his family can't be from Sydney or he'd have met *them*. Yet they must have money because Mum said she'd heard from Megan's mother that he went to school with James Logan and Hugh Parkinson. That's how he came to be in the wedding party.'

Nicole rolled her eyes. That family were incorrigible gossips! Of course, they had little else to do with their time. None of them worked.

'Thank you for that vital information,' she said ruefully.

'It *is* vital. He's a catch, sweetie. Don't let him get away.'

'See you some time tonight, Kara. Bye.' She hung up and immediately switched her phone to 'voicemail'. No more calls for her today!

'What vital information was that?' Russell asked as she slipped the phone back into her bag.

Nicole decided to be as honest as he was reputed to be.

'Kara's been asking around about you.'

'And?'

'Her mum said your family must have money because you went to school with James Logan and Hugh Parkinson.'

Russell's heart lurched at this reminder of the expensive education that had pushed his father further into debt.

'I was a scholarship boy from the country,' he said truthfully enough, not adding that such scholarships hardly touched the sides of the expenses associated with going to such a school. 'My family were far from rich. What other misleading information did she uncover?'

'Her dad said you had a good reputation in the real-estate world.'

'Well, I'd like to think that was true.'

'Yet you don't network much in a social sense.'

He flicked her a frowning glance. 'Is that comment from you, or Kara's dad?'

'Kara's dad. But Kara and I already knew you weren't big on Sydney's social scene, because we would have met you before if you were.'

'I've never been one for dinner parties. Or gallery openings. Like I said, I'm a country boy.'

'And there I was, thinking you were a playboy.'

Russell smiled. 'You're mixing me up with Hugh.'

'Yet you're good friends with him and James Logan, both of whom love socialising, not to mention the limelight. You can't open a glossy without seeing a photo of one of them.'

'We were forced to share a room together at school,' Russell explained. 'I think it was a case of opposites attracting, because we soon became firm friends. Then, after we left school, we flatted together at uni. You shouldn't judge a book by its cover, Nicole. They're both great guys.'

'If you say so.'

'So that's it, is it? No more vital information about me?'

'Pretty well.'

'You're leaving something out.'

Nicole sighed. 'OK. Kara also said you were a great catch and I wasn't to let you get away.'

'Really.'

'Look, that's Kara talking, not me. Girls like Kara think the answer to their future happiness is a seriously rich husband.'

'And you don't agree?'

'I might have. Once. Please don't be offended, but I've come to the conclusion that seriously rich guys are all arrogant, ruthless, selfish bastards with absolutely no conscience at all.'

Russell only just managed to hide his surprise at this unexpected statement. Once again, he wondered if she meant what she said. Or was she being super-clever by pretending she wasn't on the lookout for a rich husband?

'That's a rather sweeping generality, don't you think?'

'Is it? Yes, you're probably right. My bad experience with David has made me terribly cynical. I'm sure there are several seriously rich men out there somewhere who are nice. Kara's dad is a darling,' she conceded.

'And then there's me, of course,' he said with a superbly straight face.

'Just because you were once a country boy, Russell, doesn't mean you haven't been corrupted.'

'What will it take to prove to you that I'm not a playboy?'

Nicole shrugged. 'I think what happens today will speak for itself.'

'Meaning?'

'Well, you're not bringing me to your fancy bachelor pad overlooking the harbour just for breakfast, are you?'

His fancy bachelor pad…

Russell had to laugh. Life could be very perverse, no doubt about that. 'You might be in for a surprise or two.'

'I don't think so.'

'We'll see,' he said for the second time that morning.

'We certainly will,' she countered firmly.

CHAPTER FIFTEEN

'So what do you think?' Russell asked Nicole when she finally made it back to his kitchen.

He'd sent her off to inspect his modest two-bed-roomed apartment whilst he got on with breakfast, knowing that seeing was believing.

'Not quite what you were expecting?' he added with a wry smile when he saw the surprise in her face.

'Not quite,' she agreed as she slid up onto one of the two kitchen stools. 'It's no playboy pad. But I love it.'

'You *love* it?' Scepticism abounded in his reaction.

'Yes, I do,' she reaffirmed with a saucy toss of her head. 'It's in a great position, and has everything you would ever need—an *en suite* bathroom, an internal laundry with a dryer and a quite spacious kitchen. OK, so you only have the one living room, but most people don't use dining rooms these days. And the view from the balcony is incredible.'

'The very small balcony,' he pointed out. Surely she *had* to be on the make. No girl who lived the life of luxury Nicole Power had lived would rave over this modest place.

'Not *that* small,' she insisted. 'You have an outdoor

dining area on it. It's nicely private and north-facing. It must be lovely in the winter.'

'It is, actually,' he said, having not thought of his simple abode in such glowing terms before. 'Weather permitting, I sit there in the sun every morning with a cup of coffee.'

'I did wonder how you got your tan. Being a workaholic, that is,' she added with one of her bewitching smiles.

He just stared at her for a long moment before turning to pour some orange juice into a glass. 'Here. Drink this while you're waiting for the food.'

He pushed it across the breakfast bar before returning his attention to the sizzling frying-pan, his thoughts spinning. Once again, she'd surprised and confused him.

When she didn't say anything more he glanced over his shoulder to find her sitting there, slowly sipping her juice whilst watching him closely with an odd expression on her face.

'What are you thinking now?' he asked. Maybe if he kept her talking she might show her hand. He had to find out if she was being sincere, or if she was just saying what she thought he wanted her to say.

'I'm trying to work you out,' she said.

She was trying to work *him* out. Now, that was a laugh!

'What's to work out? I'm just a simple country boy who made good in the city.'

She shook her head at him, her expression wry. 'Nothing is that simple. You're certainly not. For instance, this is definitely the home of a man who isn't interested in entertaining, or impressing the ladies.'

'I did try to tell you I wasn't a playboy, but you wouldn't believe me.'

'So if you're not a playboy, or a show pony, then who

is the man who bought our extremely ostentatious home in Belleview Hill?' she persisted. 'If you were the sort of man who wanted a flashy place, you'd already be living in one. You wouldn't be living here. So tell me, why *did* you buy it?'

Russell jerked his eyes back to the frying-pan lest she glimpse the surge of vengeful fury which her provocative question evoked. The temptation to throw the truth at her was intense.

Because your rotten father was responsible for my wonderful father killing himself, he could hear himself saying. *I vowed to one day take everything that bastard held dear. That's why I bought his home. And why I bedded you, his darling daughter, last night.*

But he didn't say any of those words. Because he knew that would be the end of it. The end of him and Nicole.

As much as Russell craved revenge, it seemed he craved her more. He couldn't bear the thought of her exiting his life. Couldn't bear the prospect of never holding her in his arms again, never feeling what she could make him feel.

'Russell?' she probed. 'Aren't you going to answer me?'

'Sorry. I find it hard to talk and cook at the same time. The thing is, I actually bought your place as an investment,' he lied as he busied himself serving up their bacon and eggs. 'I'd heard it was for sale and hoped to get a bargain. Admittedly, I *was* planning to live there for a while. That way I wouldn't have to pay capital-gains tax when I eventually sold it. But James has already offered me a ridiculously large sum, which I am seriously considering.' This part wasn't a lie. James had made the offer when they'd had drinks at the house the other night. 'Now that James is married with a baby on the way, he's looking for a good-sized family home.'

'Megan is expecting?'

'You didn't know?'

'No.'

Russell could have kicked himself. 'Keep it to yourself then, will you?'

'Of course. Wow! Your friend has just gone up in my estimation. Let's face it, wealthy men don't have to marry girls they get pregnant these days. He must actually love her.'

Russell adopted a poker face. 'I did tell you he was a good guy. Still, don't relay any of this to that gossipy girlfriend of yours. Now, where would you like to eat breakfast? In here or out on the balcony?'

'Definitely the balcony.'

'That was ever so nice,' Nicole complimented after she'd finished eating. 'You are a very good cook.'

'Not really. Bacon and eggs and toast are pretty foolproof.'

Nicole laughed. 'Don't you believe it. I could ruin them. I'm a dreadful cook.'

'Lack of practice, I suppose.'

'You're right there. I'm totally useless around the house.' From the time her mother married Alistair neither of them had had to lift a finger. Nicole had thought her life was wonderful at the time, not realising how spoiled and lazy she'd become.

She had to admire Russell. He'd made his own way in life, made his own fortune. Yet despite his material success, he wasn't a show-pony. She liked that about him. A lot.

Her qualms over his being rich were gradually fading as well, Russell's solid work ethics and simple lifestyle showing a man of character and depth. Surprising, though, that he hadn't married. Possibly he hadn't met the right girl. More likely, his priority had been making money. She wondered what was in his past which had fuelled his ambition. Nicole realised from her own experiences that past history was a great influence on the person you became. No one was immune to carrying emotional baggage. She'd had her fair share.

Still, if she was going to keep on sleeping with this man, she really should find out some more about him.

'Tell me about your family, Russell,' she asked. 'Do you have any brothers and sisters?'

'Nope. I was the only offspring.'

'You said you were a farmer's son. Whereabouts is your dad's farm?'

He didn't answer straight away, taking a sip of coffee first.

'Dad passed away a long time ago.'

'How sad. He must have been quite young.'

'Only forty-five.'

'What did he die of? Cancer?'

Once again he seemed reluctant to answer.

'He shot himself,' he said at last, the baldness of his statement at odds with the pain in his face.

'Oh. Russell… Oh, how awful for you.'

Russell was startled when her eyes actually filled with tears. Her compassion moved him, for it seemed sincere. Suddenly, he wanted to tell her more. Not the whole horrible truth, of course. Just…more.

'It was,' he admitted. 'The drought was very bad at

the time and Dad had gotten himself into serious debt. Mum said afterwards that he'd become very depressed. When the farm was repossessed, he lost the will to live.'

'I…I don't know what to say…'

Her soft words of sympathy got to Russell even more than her tears. Every muscle in his body tightened, the control he usually had over his emotions in real danger of disintegrating.

'It's all right,' he ground out through clenched teeth.

'No, it's not all right. Suicide is never all right. Your poor dad. And your poor mum.'

Hell, he'd made a mistake, going down this path. He could feel himself beginning to unravel, like long rows of knitting being wrenched undone. Soon, there would be nothing left of him but a twisted-up mess.

'Mum's fine now,' he said, pulling himself together with a supreme effort of will. 'She married again. Another farmer. They live out at Gulgong, near Mudgee.'

'Whilst you came to Sydney and became a workaholic.'

He shrugged. 'There are worse things I could have become. But enough about me. You promised to tell me why you want to go back to Thailand.'

Nicole knew he was deliberately changing the subject. And she didn't blame him. Remembering the past could be very painful. She'd been terribly hurt by David's betrayal, plus the discovery that her stepfather was equally conscienceless. But neither of those events compared with Russell losing his dad in such a tragic way. It was patently obvious that his father's suicide had affected him deeply.

'Come, now,' he chided when she remained silent. 'Tell the truth and shame the devil.'

She smiled, then shrugged. 'The truth is I met this truly amazing woman when I was in Bangkok. She runs an orphanage full of sweet but very underprivileged children. They have nothing in the way of material possessions yet they're so happy. They made me ashamed of all the things that had been lavished on me over the years. Anyway, I promised her that after I'd collected my belongings, I'd go back and help her out for a while.' She almost told him that she was going to sell all her jewellery to raise money to buy the children some much needed items, but didn't want to sound like some martyrish saint. Nicole knew she was far from that.

The expression on Russell's face still showed true surprise, Nicole accepted that it *was* an unlikely thing for a girl like her to be doing. Kara's reaction had been similar.

'What kind of help are you talking about?' he asked. 'Money?'

'Money would certainly go a long way to solving a lot of Julie's problems.'

'In that case why not just send this woman some? You don't have to go over there personally.'

'Yes,' she said firmly. 'I do. I promised the children. Look, I'm not going to stay there forever. I'll be back in Sydney in the New Year to look for a job.'

His eyebrows shot upwards. 'A job?'

Nicole could not help bristling at his constant surprise. 'I am employable, you know. I have a degree in marketing. I worked for Power Mortgages for nearly two years,' she said, her pride not mentioning that she hadn't worked in their marketing section. 'I only left a few months ago.'

* * *

Once again, Russell struggled to hide his emotions in front of her. He'd been on the verge of changing his mind about Nicole's character, speculating that she could be so different from what he'd been imagining. Not on the make, not selfish and not content to live an idle existence.

Her announcement, however, that she'd actually worked for her father's company for nearly two years, clearly in the marketing section, had floored him.

She had to have known her father's business practices; in fact, she must have condoned them.

Any guilt he'd begun harbouring over his ruthless behaviour last night was instantly banished, replaced once again by that coldly implacable resolve to continue with his vengeful mission... He would harness his passion for her to good effect, making magnificent love to her till she changed her mind about going overseas; till she fell madly in love with him; till she agreed to marry him.

Not that he intended to actually marry her. Hopefully, by the time she accepted his proposal, this insane desire would have burned itself out.

'Why did you leave?' he asked, pleased at his casual tone.

'I couldn't bear to stay in Sydney after what happened with David. I...I had to get away.'

So she had just upped and gone overseas for months on end, no doubt having everything paid for by Daddy.

And now she was going overseas again. Still using Daddy's money, Russell presumed. He recalled her saying something to her mother last night about not needing to be sent any more money.

Her looking for a job in the New Year was obviously not a necessity, just something to fill her time. This mission of mercy might be much of the same. One did need a purpose in life.

Like revenge...

'When are you thinking of leaving for Thailand?' he asked.

'I was hoping to fly out by the middle of the week.'

'That soon.'

'It all depends on the flights available.'

'You must realise I don't want you to go,' he said, his eyes locking with hers. 'Stay here in Sydney with me and I'll give your friend more money than she knows what to do with.'

Nicole should not have been shocked, but she was.

For a while there, she'd forgotten who she was dealing with. Forgotten what life had taught her. That rich men did not always follow society's rules.

Russell might live a simple lifestyle on the surface, but he was not a simple man. You didn't achieve as much as he had in such a short space of time without being very tunnel-visioned, and without becoming somewhat ruthless in the process.

'That's nothing short of blackmail,' she scolded.

His smile had a wickedly sexy edge to it. 'And that's not an answer.'

Nicole's heart quickened as temptation took hold. The passion in his eyes was powerfully persuasive, promising more pleasures of the kind she'd tasted last night. If she stayed here in Sydney she could spend every night in his bed, being swept away into his erotic world.

'How much money are we looking at?' she couldn't resist asking.

'As much as it takes.'

He must really want her a lot. Nicole could not help

feeling flattered. But along with the seductive flattery lay annoyance that he would think he could buy her.

'I'm sorry,' she said tartly. 'But I'm not for sale.'

'What a pity. It's just as well, then,' he went on as he rose to his feet, 'that I have other means of persuasion.'

Nicole had anticipated this moment. What she hadn't anticipated was that, by the time he came to seduce her again, she would feel so angry with him.

Why, then, didn't she struggle when he pulled her up off the chair and into his arms? Why not turn her mouth away? Why not slap his arrogantly presumptuous face?

Her vulnerability to him should have been humiliating. There *were* a few moments of mortification. But that was before his lips went to work with a vengeance. In no time she didn't care what kind of man he was, as long as he kept on kissing her.

She could not think, could hardly breathe.

He disposed of her dress in no time, then her panties. Once again, she stood naked before him. But in the daylight this time, in the sunshine.

He stepped back, his eyes narrowing as they travelled over her by now quivering nudity. 'You are way too beautiful for your own good, do you know that?'

She had ceased to know anything some time back.

'Women like you have brought down countries.'

All of a sudden he bent to scoop her up into his arms, crushing her against his chest as he carried her inside. 'I apologise for making that insulting offer,' he ground out as he forged down the short hallway into his bedroom. 'But you must know how I feel about you. I can't bear the thought of our being parted so soon after finding you. I'm crazy about you, Nicole.'

Her head whirled at his impassioned words, then

whirled some more when he literally tossed her into the middle of his bed.

'We won't talk any more of your going to Thailand today,' he said as he began stripping off his clothes with urgent haste. 'We'll just enjoy each other like we did last night. Without any thought of the future. Just for the pleasure of the moment.'

Their mating was fast and furious, their satisfaction simultaneous. Afterwards they clung to each other, their breathing still ragged. Nicole sobbed when he withdrew, not wanting him to leave her, even for the short space of time it took him to go to the bathroom.

When he came back, he lay down beside her and gently pushed her tangled hair back from her face.

'It's no use, my darling,' he said as he caressed her still flushed cheek. 'I simply can't let you go.'

Nicole stiffened in his arms.

'I'm going to Thailand with you.'

She just stared up at him.

'What's the problem now?' he demanded to know. 'You don't want me to go with you?'

She did. Of course she did. But something didn't feel right. Everything was happening too quickly. Last night. And now this.

They weren't in love. How could they be? Love didn't happen that quickly.

Or did it?

OK, so she'd never experienced anything like what she had last night. Or just now.

But that wasn't love. Not yet, anyway.

'That's not the point,' she said, trying to be sensible. 'I only met you a few days ago. Look, like I said earlier,

I won't be gone forever. If you like, I'll come back for Christmas.'

'Christmas is more than a month away. I can't do without you for that long.'

'I'm afraid you'll just have to.'

'I can't. I'll go crazy.'

'*This* is crazy,' she said, even as she felt herself weakening. 'You can't just drop everything and fly off overseas at a moment's notice. I thought you said you were a workaholic.'

'I was, till I met you. I'm not at work today, yet Sunday is top dog in the real-estate business. You might not have noticed but I texted a message to my office to say that I wouldn't be in today. Then I turned off my cellphone. Trust me when I say that's a first in several years.'

Nicole frowned.

Trust. That was the bottom line. There'd been something about Russell when she'd first met him which she didn't trust. He'd come across as hard and predatory, a rich man who would stop at nothing to get what he wanted. Which was her, at this point in time.

But for how long?

'Don't say no,' he said, his eyes going all smoky as he cupped her face and his head began to descend.

She just couldn't resist him.

'All right,' she said, and surrendered her mouth to his.

CHAPTER SIXTEEN

'YOU'RE spoiling me,' Nicole said when Russell came into the bathroom with her freshly laundered dress and underwear.

She was lying back in the bath, wallowing in the relaxing warmth and trying not to worry over her growing addiction to this man. Truly, she simply could not keep her hands off him.

Russell hadn't joined her in the bath, claiming that if he did she'd turn him on again and they'd never make it to dinner. Instead he'd headed for the other bathroom, where he'd showered, shaved and dressed before returning in a smart grey lounge suit and an open-necked white shirt that highlighted his olive skin.

'Out of that bath, madam,' he ordered, 'and into these clothes, post-haste. I'm starving.'

'I don't think I have the energy for dinner,' she complained.

'I don't wonder. Come on. Up and out of there. Our booking is for seven-thirty and it's already ten to seven.'

Russell left the room, closing the door after him, leaving Nicole to sigh, then drag herself out of the water. With only lipstick and a small comb in her evening bag, she didn't take long to get ready. Fifteen minutes later they were in the car and on their way across the bridge, Russell having chosen a well-known seafood restaurant on the quay for dinner. It was called Neptune's, after the god of the sea, and positioned on the upper level of a renovated warehouse. Its spectacular view of the harbour meant it was very popular, though the exorbitant prices did keep the clientele exclusive.

Nicole rather suspected Russell had chosen it to impress her.

She didn't mention she'd been there before. Because let's face it, she thought, there weren't too many restaurants in Sydney—even the most expensive ones—which she hadn't graced at one time or other.

'Rather than tell you how beautiful you look,' he said with an admiring glance her way, 'I will just say that you are the only girl I've ever been with who looks fantastic, *au naturel*.'

Being a typical female, Nicole focused her mind on the other girls he'd been with, rather than his very nice compliment.

'And how many other girls have there been?'

This time, his glance carried a rather smug smile. 'You're jealous.'

'Don't avoid the question. How many girlfriends have there been before me?'

'So you're happy to call yourself my girlfriend now?'

'Russell McClain, I've just spent the entire day in bed with you. If I'm not your girlfriend then I'd have to be the biggest slut of all time. Which I'm not. On top of that, I've agreed to your coming to Thailand with me. That rather smacks of some kind of relationship, don't you think? Now answer my question, please.'

'Don't get your knickers in a knot. Sorry, but I can't tell you an exact number. I don't keep count. But I would hazard a guess at forty. Maybe fifty?'

'Good lord, you *are* a playboy!'

'Nicole, I'm thirty-six years old. At that age, I don't think that fifty's too unacceptable, do you?'

'I guess not. How many were you in love with?'

'None.'

'*Really?*'

'Really.'

Now, why did that make her feel so good?

Because you think he's in love with you, that's why. You think you're special. You think…you think too darned much sometimes, Nicole Power.

'Is that why you've never got married?' she heard herself ask before she could snatch it back.

The silence in the car was excruciating. And embarrassing.

Nicole wished she'd kept her silly mouth shut. The last thing you started talking about at the beginning of a relationship was marriage. It made men run a mile, which was the last thing she wanted Russell to do.

'Marriage hasn't fitted into my workaholic lifestyle,' he said at last. 'I will definitely consider it, when I meet the right person.'

His head turned and so did hers. Their eyes met, his glittering at her with a thousand possessive lights.

'I don't want to scare you off, lovely Nicole, with premature talk about love and marriage. For now, I just want to get to know you better. And to never let you out of my sight,' he added with another of his wickedly sexy smiles.

The subject of marriage was dropped after that, Russell turning the conversation away to her seafood preferences. By the time the car was safely stowed in a small car park at the back of the quay, both agreed that lobster was their favourite, with oysters and prawns high on the list.

But her heart was racing all the while.

When Russell opened the passenger door and took her hand, that same heart lurched tellingly. When he smiled down at her, she smiled fatuously back. When he pulled her up onto her slightly shaky legs, she was more than ready to be kissed.

He took his time, only letting her go when she was decidedly light-headed. Nicole was glad of his supporting hand as they walked towards the restaurant. Her legs were as jelly-like as her brain.

When Russell's step faltered she glanced up to find him frowning.

'Is something wrong?' she asked.

His sigh sounded frustrated. 'I have an awful suspicion that Hugh might be here tonight at Neptune's. His car's parked just over there.'

Nicole's gaze followed his to land on a shiny red Ferrari. How typical of Hugh Parkinson, she thought tartly.

'But there are lots of restaurants within walking distance of this car park. He could be at any one of them.'

'He's very partial to seafood.'

'Lots of seafood restaurants, too,' she pointed out.

'True. It would be bad luck if he had chosen ours.'

She stopped and stared up at him. 'Why bad luck?'

'You're wearing the same dress you were wearing last night. It's a possibility Hugh might be with one of the bridesmaids from the wedding. He was zeroing in on her before we left. They'll know we spent last night together, and all today as well.'

Whilst Nicole was touched that Russell was protecting her reputation, she wasn't inclined to change their plans for the likes of Hugh Parkinson, who probably slept with a different girl every other week. His bed-partner count would be mammoth compared to Russell's.

'Don't be silly,' she said. 'Why would Hugh care if we spent the night together? Why should anyone care?'

He still looked worried for some reason.

'Come on,' she said, and tugged at his hand. 'I'm not traipsing around a lot of other places in these killer heels. If Hugh's at Neptune's, then so be it.'

Russell just knew Hugh would be there. And he was, sitting at the best table in the house, looking rakishly handsome and sipping a glass of no doubt outrageously expensive red wine.

That he was alone was the only surprise.

Hugh didn't see them till they were shown to the second-best table in the house, not far from his.

'Hello, Hugh,' Russell said before Hugh could give voice to his astonishment. 'Fancy meeting you here. I don't need to introduce you to Nicole, do I? I gather that you've already met.'

As always Hugh quickly found his cool, and his charm. 'Indeed, we have,' he agreed with one of his woman-winning smiles. 'But it's some time since we've actually spoken. Life must be treating you well, Nicole. You're looking exceptionally lovely tonight.'

'Thank you,' Nicole said as she sat down, a faint flush coming to her cheeks.

'You must tell me what you've been up to since we last met. But not from that distance. I insist you join me for dinner. And you, too, Russ, of course,' he added nonchalantly.

Russell's teeth clenched down hard in his jaw. He'd seen Hugh go into action with members of the opposite sex before, and they invariably succumbed to his charms. The thought that he might turn Nicole's head evoked a jab of jealousy which was as dark as it was powerful.

'Only on condition you don't flirt with my girl-friend,' Russell pronounced, his eyes throwing dagger-like warnings at his friend.

Hugh's eyebrows lifted. 'Girlfriend? My, but you are a fast worker. I got the impression you didn't even know Nicole before last night.'

'Haven't you heard of whirlwind romances?'

'Unfortunately, yes. My father thrives on them. But I never took you for being someone so impulsive. No casting aspersions at you, lovely Nicole. If ever anyone could knock my old mate there for six, it would be you.'

Russell was grateful that Nicole would not grasp the wicked irony in this last statement. He still considered grabbing her hand and dragging her away from what was going to be a very awkward dinner, but knew that would look odd. He had no option but to brave it out. But inside he was furious with Hugh. He was supposed to be his friend, damn it!

Russell decided to deflect the conversation away from his relationship with Nicole as quickly as possible.

'It's not like you to eat alone,' he directed at Hugh once the three of them were seated together and extra placings had been set. 'What happened to what's-her-name from last night?'

Hugh wrinkled his nose. 'You were right. Far too clingy. So what would you two like to drink? Some of my red, or should I order some champagne to celebrate your getting together?'

'Some champagne would be lovely,' Nicole said politely whilst Russell was still gnashing his teeth. He'd get that troublemaking devil later. Nicole was sure to go to the ladies' at some stage.

And when she did...

The champagne was delivered with the kind of swift service that a billionaire's son and heir invariably commanded.

'To Nicole and Russ,' Hugh toasted with a supercilious smile as he clinked his champagne flute with Nicole's.

Russell eyed his friend coldly. 'There's no need to overdo things. We're not engaged, just dating.'

'But just dating is a big step for you, Russ. He's a dreadful workaholic, you know, Nicole.'

'Yes, so he's told me,' she replied with a quick smile Russell's way. 'But he didn't go to work today.'

'I rather gathered that,' Hugh replied with a telling glance at Nicole's dress. 'Speaking of engagements,' he went on, 'the last time we met was at your and David Porter's engagement party. That obviously didn't work out.'

'No,' Nicole agreed, the smile fading from her face.

Russell could have killed Hugh. 'He was a bastard,' Russell snapped.

'Men can be bastards,' Hugh agreed, and looked Russell straight in the eye.

'Takes one to know one,' Russell countered.

Hugh dropped the ironic remarks after that, instead using his natural charm over dinner, not to flirt with Nicole, but to try to get her to talk about herself. But she cleverly deflected his personal probings, keeping the chit-chat to general topics.

Russell sat back in the main, grateful that Nicole wasn't

one of those girls who confided everything to everyone. She didn't reveal any details about their affair so far. Neither did she mention her coming trip to Thailand, or the fact that Russell had offered to go with her.

Russell admired people who kept private things private.

Every now and then she threw him a glance that was just for him; a warm and intimate glance which gave him great satisfaction.

By the time she excused herself to go to the ladies room, he no longer felt any urgent need to have a go at Hugh. Nicole was handling him just fine all by herself. Russell felt something close to pride as he watched her walk away from the table, her beautiful head held high on her long, elegant neck. Several male heads turned to look at her, their expressions openly admiring.

It came to Russell then that marriage to Nicole would have a lot of benefits and bonuses. Not only would it feed his craving for revenge, but he would also acquire an exciting bed-partner, plus an accomplished hostess and the most exquisite piece of arm candy that any man could possess.

'What in bloody hell do you think you're doing?' Hugh snapped.

Russell took a second or two before answering. 'With regard to what?'

'You know what. Hell, Russ, what you're doing to that girl isn't right. Surely you can see that.'

'I see that I'm finally getting some sort of satisfaction after all these years.'

Hugh shook his head at Russ. 'Look, I don't give a damn about what you did to Alistair Power. I don't care if he's rotting away in some Third World hell-hole. But

Nicole's an innocent pawn in all this. She wasn't responsible for your father's death.'

Russell's face darkened. 'That's what you think. I'll have you know that she worked for Power Mortgages in their marketing section till a few months ago. She must have known what was going on there, so don't give me any of that "innocent pawn" crap. Oh, and I doubt Alistair Power is in some Third World hell-hole,' he sneered. 'He's been supporting Nicole's overseas jaunts since she broke off her engagement to Porter. Takes a lot of money to float around the world for several months.'

'All right, all right. I get your point. But damn it all, Russ, enough's enough. You've had the pleasure of seducing your enemy's daughter, *in* your enemy's bed, no doubt.'

'How did you guess?'

'Because you're twisted. But you're not cruel, Russ. You've never been cruel. Seduction is one thing. Making the girl fall in love with you is another.'

'You think she's fallen in love with me?'

'Only a blind man wouldn't notice!' Why else wouldn't she have paid any attention to *him*? 'She can't take her eyes off you for long.'

'That's good,' Russell said, nodding rather smugly. 'That's very good. Women in love are usually amenable to a marriage proposal.'

Hugh stared at him. 'What? You're going to ask her to *marry* you? Are you insane?'

'No,' Russ said, his eyes hardening. 'I'm just doing what I've waited sixteen years to do.'

Hugh could not believe what he was hearing. 'So when are you going to break her heart with the truth?' he threw at his friend. 'On your wedding night?'

'No. Never.'

'Never!'

'I want her to be my wife, Hugh. For the rest of my life.'

'So where does the revenge bit come in?'

'What do you mean?'

'It's not revenge, if she never finds out the truth.'

'That depends on how you look at it. Being with her has already given me great satisfaction.'

'Yes, but what kind of satisfaction? Are you sure this idea of yours is instigated by revenge, Russ? Maybe you've fallen in love with her.'

'Don't be ridiculous!' Russell denied heatedly.

Too heatedly, Hugh thought. Nicole was an exceptionally beautiful girl, with a way about her which any man would find enchanting.

'So how long before you're going to pop the question?' Hugh asked, his eyes continually scanning the corner of the restaurant where the ladies' room was located. No sign of Nicole yet.

'I'm going to propose when we're in Thailand together.'

'What's this? You're going to Thailand together! *When?*'

'As soon as it can be arranged.'

'For how long?'

'For as long as it takes.'

'What about your business?'

'It'll survive without me. Properties practically sell themselves at this time of year. Speaking of real estate, it seems the Belleview Hill house doesn't find favour with Nicole, so I've decided to sell the place to James. Remember how he offered to buy it the other night?'

'Yeah, but you said no.'

'That was then and this is now. I'm going to text him tomorrow and agree to his offer.'

'You're deadly serious about all this, aren't you?'

'Yes, and if you say anything to Nicole, that will be the end of our friendship.'

Hugh looked into Russell's eyes and knew he meant it.

'I won't say a word,' he said with a resigned sigh. 'Scout's honour.'

'There's only one problem with that,' Russell growled.

'What?'

'You're no scout!'

CHAPTER SEVENTEEN

'HEAVENS!' Kara exclaimed after Nicole told her everything later that night. Levering herself up on one elbow, she glanced over at where Nicole was lying on the other twin bed. 'It sounds like he's really fallen for you.'

'I hope so. Because I've fallen for him. Big time!'

Kara flopped back down on her pillow. 'Who would have thought when I dragged you off to Megan's wedding, you'd actually find yourself that seriously rich husband you need?'

Nicole shot her a reproving look. 'Kara, for pity's sake don't go saying anything like that to other people. I didn't fall for Russell because he's rich. In fact, that's the one thing which worries me about him. That, and that annoying friend of his.'

'Who? Hugh Parkinson?'

'Who else?'

'I think he's yummy.'

'More like crummy. The man's a compulsive womaniser.'

'I know. But somehow that only adds to his charm. I would imagine women find him a challenge. And, of course, he'd have to be very good in bed. Practice does make perfect.'

Nicole had to concede Hugh did have charm. And he was impossibly good-looking. But no man could match her Russell. He was all man, a simply incredible lover.

'I wonder how Megan's enjoying her honeymoon,' Kara said out of the blue.

'I would imagine very much so,' Nicole replied. How could she not be? She was with the man she loved, and who loved her.

'She's pregnant, you know,' Kara said unexpectedly.

Nicole frowned. 'How long have you known that? You never said anything before the wedding.'

'I overheard Mum discussing it with Dad today. Megan's only about two months gone. The wedding was a real rush job. Dad thinks it's all a bit suspect. I can't imagine why. Do you think there's anything strange in a man marrying his pregnant girlfiend?'

'Not at all. I think it's sweet.'

'Same here.'

'He must really love her.'

'Did you doubt it?'

'Rich men can be ruthless devils,' Nicole said.

'That's exactly what Dad said, though I can't see how marrying Megan when she got preggers was ruthless. He's an old cynic sometimes, is Dad. The trouble is, he's often right. He's shuttled off a few of the guys I've dated over the years after finding out they were fortune-hunters. Luckily, Leyton's loaded, so no trouble there.'

'Are you in love with Leyton?'

'Nah, but he's fun to be with. I might keep him around for a while. I'm in no hurry to marry. Still, when I do, it will have to be to someone with plenty of money. That way, I'll know he likes me for myself.'

'I hope Russell doesn't ever think I'm after him for his money.'

'How can he possibly think that when you're selling all of your lovely jewellery tomorrow? Which, by the way, I think is crazy, when you have a wealthy lover eating out of your hand. You'd only have to ask and he'd give you whatever you want. Why be a penniless martyr when you can become a well-heeled mistress?'

'Are you serious? No way would I ever become a kept woman. Look, Kara, there's something I have to warn you about. Russell doesn't know my true financial circumstances. Or about my selling my jewellery tomorrow. I've let him think I do have some money of my own.'

'Why on earth did you do that?'

'It seemed like a good idea at the time. Pride, I guess.'

'Mmm. You'd better tell him the truth. It's not a good thing to lie, especially about money. He'll have to know eventually.'

'I suppose so. I'll tell him tomorrow, over lunch. He's going to pick me up here at one.'

'Mmm. On second thoughts, maybe you shouldn't tell him about the jewellery. He might not understand. But you should let him know that you don't have a permanent private income, that whatever money you have will eventually run out.'

'That shouldn't be a problem. I've already told him I'm going to get a job in the New Year.'

'Good thinking.'

'It's the truth!'

'You won't have to worry about a job when you become Mrs Russell McClain.'

'Let's not get ahead of ourselves here. Like Russell told his friend tonight, we're not engaged. We're just dating.'

'But he's going to propose, from what you've said.'

'Maybe. But not yet.'

'Will you be moving in with him when you come back from Bangkok?'

'I will, if he asks me.'

'He will. Now, what are you going to wear tomorrow? Don't tell me. Jeans, I'll bet.'

'What's wrong with jeans? It's only lunch, and probably only at a local café.'

Kara looked exasperated. 'At least wear a decent shirt with them. I could lend you one if needs be. And some decent accessories. I have something for every occasion.'

Nicole didn't doubt it. That girl's wardrobe had long extended into one of her mother's many guest rooms. 'Kara, I really need to go to sleep now. I'm tired.'

'There's no sleep for the wicked.'

'I'm not wicked.'

'You have been since you met lover-boy, from what you told me.'

'Kara!'

'OK, OK,' Kara said, and snapped off her bedside lamp.

Nicole did likewise. But she didn't go to sleep. She kept thinking about Russell and how much she missed him already. She hadn't wanted to come back to Kara's place straight after dinner. She'd wanted to stay with him. Wanted to be back in his arms again. At least for a while.

Something had stopped her from giving in to temptation.

That something had been the momentary look she'd caught in Hugh Parkinson's eyes when he'd first seen them together. He hadn't just been surprised. He'd been appalled.

Nicole believed she knew why.

He thought she was a gold-digger. That was why he'd flirted with her so shamelessly—to see if he could seduce her away from his friend; to show her up to Russell.

Nicole imagined that men such as Hugh Parkinson were extremely cynical about some women's motivations. It couldn't be easy being the only son and heir of one of Australia's richest men. Hugh would have become a target from the moment he grew up.

Still, he had no right to try to poison, or spoil, Russell's relationships. Flirting with her, then bringing up her engagement to David, had not been very nice.

She suspected Russell must have said something to him whilst she was in the powder room. Because Hugh had been different when she'd returned.

Less provocative. Less chatty all round.

But there'd still been flashes of concern in his eyes when he'd looked at her.

Nothing, Nicole accepted with a weary sigh, was going to change Hugh's mind about why she was dating his friend. Hopefully, he would not be able to sway Russell where she was concerned.

Still, Hugh's distrust was perfectly understandable.

Her association with the name Power meant she would inevitably be labelled greedy and conscienceless by people who didn't know her. Her lifestyle in the past didn't help, either. Hugh probably saw her as a spoiled rich bitch who now no longer had the means to carry on her party-going lifestyle. *Ergo*, she was on the lookout for a wealthy boyfriend who could keep her in the manner to which she had become accustomed. He would not believe that she genuinely cared for Russell for himself, or that she was no longer interested in living the high life.

Her not telling Russell her true financial circumstances right from the beginning began to seriously worry Nicole. What would happen if he found out she'd lied to him? She would just die if he ever thought she was a fortune-hunter.

'Will you stop all that sighing?' Kara snapped through the darkness.

'Sorry.'

'If you don't go to sleep soon, you're going to have dark rings under your eyes tomorrow.'

Nicole had to smile. 'And that would never do,' she said.

'Absolutely not!'

CHAPTER EIGHTEEN

RUSSELL spent the following morning putting his business affairs in order so that he could go to Thailand. None of his branch managers seemed worried by his decision to have a 'holiday'. They all thought it was way past time for him to have a break.

Despite reassuring Nicole that he would not be missed at this time of year, Russell couldn't help feeling some pique at their cavalier attitude. Of course, he did always hire the best, so he shouldn't have been too disgruntled. But when the people in the Bondi office— where he spent most of his time—seemed only too happy to see the back of him for a while, Russell was forced to take a good look at himself.

He was not the easiest of bosses, he realised as he drove towards Kara's house to pick up Nicole. He was often difficult and demanding, not always overly understanding, perhaps, that his employees had private lives. On the plus side, he paid his employees extremely well. Surely, he had the right to expect them to work hard.

Russell gave himself a severe mental shake. He had to stop this. Stop questioning himself at every turn. Hugh had put all sorts of doubts into his head last night. He'd spent a restless night, getting only a few hours' sleep.

He was not a cruel man, he told himself. Perhaps a little hard. OK, a lot hard.

But that was not his fault. That was Power's fault!

There was no way he could change now. He was what he was.

Kara's home came into view, a typical old-money mansion, sitting on an extra-large block with a high brick wall around it and lots of overgrown trees in the grounds. Probably built in the thirties, the house was two-storeyed and colonial in architecture with wrap-around verandas on both levels.

Russell drove straight in, the gates obviously having been left open in anticipation of his arrival. His car crunched to a halt next to the front steps, his dark mood lifting at the thought of seeing Nicole.

But it wasn't Nicole who answered the front doorbell. It was her friend, Kara, looking rather subdued.

'Russell. Hi,' she said in a low-keyed voice. 'Look, I'm not sure Nickie will be able to go to lunch with you. She's very upset.'

'What about?' The thought that Hugh might have rung Nicole screamed into Russell's head.

'I…I don't think I can tell you that.'

'Nothing to do with me, is it?' he demanded to know.

Kara looked taken aback. 'No. Not at all. Look, I'll go tell Nickie you're here. It might do her good to get out, poor love. Come inside.'

Russell waited in the hallway whilst Kara hurried up the impressive central staircase and disappeared from view. A couple of minutes later, Nicole appeared at the top of the stairs, dressed in dark blue jeans and a white shirt. She hesitated slightly before slowly walking down, one hand on the banister. Her face was pale, her eyes puffy and red-rimmed.

Russell's whole chest squeezed tight at the evidence of some very prolonged weeping.

'Nicole, darling,' he said, moving towards her. 'What is it? What's happened?' His mind automatically jumped to the assumption of an accident of some kind. Some tragedy. Maybe her mother had been killed. Or her father.

Strangely, this last thought didn't give him any pleasure at all. His only concern was for Nicole.

'I…I've had a shock,' she choked out. 'Something personal.'

He took both her hands in his. 'Surely you can tell me.'

Tears welled up in her eyes again. 'I'm not sure you'd understand. Or care.'

'How can you say that?'

When her head drooped forward, her hair fell around her face. 'If I tell you, you'll find out that I deliberately deceived you,' she said brokenly. 'You'll probably believe what Hugh thinks of me. That I'm some kind of gold-digger.'

He tipped her chin up with a gentle finger. 'How could I possibly ever think that of the beautiful girl who couldn't be bought?'

She began to cry then, with deep, wrenching sobs. Russell groaned, then pulled her to him, his arms wrapping tightly around her, his own heart breaking at her unhappiness.

He didn't say a word. He just let her cry whilst he struggled to come to terms with his own emotions.

Hugh was right, he finally accepted. He *had* fallen

in love with this girl. No matter what she was, no matter *who* she was.

He loved her.

When a worried-looking Kara materialised at the top of the stairs Russell waved her away, then continued to just hold Nicole till her sobs eventually subsided. Once she was quiet in his arms he held her away from him.

'I want you to go get your handbag,' he said gently, but firmly. 'We're going to have lunch.'

She glanced up at him, her lovely eyes redder than ever. 'But I can't go out looking like this!'

'Yes, you can. Put some sunglasses on. We obviously have to talk and I don't want to do it here.'

She still looked unsure.

'Kara!' Russell called up the stairs. 'Are you there?'

'Yes,' Kara replied, so quickly that she must have been very close by. Probably eavesdropping.

'Could you bring down Nicole's handbag and some sunglasses, please? I think she need a breath of fresh air. And a bite to eat.'

'Right away.'

Kara brought the handbag and glasses down in a flash, her manner much more carefree than earlier. 'Don't forget what I told you, sweetie,' she said as she handed them over. 'I'm only too happy to buy you-know-what from you. For good money, too.'

'All right,' Nicole replied wanly, leaving Russell none the wiser.

'What's you-know-what?' he asked as soon as he had Nicole alone in his car.

She slanted him a worried glance before shrugging in a rather defeated fashion. 'She's talking about my jewellery.'

Russell frowned. 'You're selling Kara some of your jewellery?'

'Not some. All.'

'*All*. But why?'

'To raise money.'

'For the orphanage?'

'Yes.'

Russell didn't know what to feel at this news. Admiration for her, or guilt that he'd ever thought her selfish and materialistic?

Guilt won hands down.

'You don't have any money, do you?' he said.

'Not much. I raised some by selling a few of my clothes. Enough for the return ticket to Thailand and a bit left over to live on whilst I'm there. But I needed the money from my jewellery to do what I wanted at the orphanage.'

Russell didn't think his guilt could get any worse, but it just had. The spoiled girl whom he'd imagined living a life of luxury off her daddy's money had been reduced to selling her clothes!

'Why didn't you tell me any of this?'

Her smile was sad. 'Pride, I guess.'

Pride. Yes, he understood about pride. He recalled how she'd refused to let her mother send her any money. That wasn't just pride. That was character—and guts.

'I didn't want you to know I was poor,' she went on. 'I didn't want you to think I might be after your money.'

'I never thought that for a moment,' he lied. 'But none of this explains why you were so upset just now. Didn't Kara say she was going to buy your jewellery?'

'Yes. But not for what I'd hoped to get.'

'Second-hand jewellery only ever sells for a fraction of what it's worth, Nicole.'

'Yes,' she said ruefully. 'Especially if it's fake.'

'Fake!'

Russell just stared at her.

'Kara's dad lined up a friend of his in the jewellery trade to come to the house this morning. He said the man would make me a fair offer. Unfortunately, he refused to make any offer at all. He said he only dealt in genuine gems.'

'What about the emerald pendant and earrings you wore at the wedding?' He could have sworn they were real.

'The man said the emeralds were extremely good fakes, but fakes all the same. Yet they were a present, specially made for my twenty-first birthday.'

'That's terrible, Nicole.' But typical of Alistair Power, he thought bitterly. The man couldn't lie straight in a bed. 'I can understand why you were so upset.'

'I didn't cry for the money so much, though I am very disappointed. It was the feeling of betrayal. Of being taken for a fool. Even after all he's done, deep down, I always believed Alistair loved me.'

'You call your father by his first name?'

Nicole looked surprised. 'Alistair Power is not my father.'

'Not your father,' Russell repeated, trying not to look as if he'd just been poleaxed.

'I took his name when my mother married him. He's my stepfather.'

Her stepfather!

'I used to think he was wonderful,' she went on, tears pricking at her eyes once more. 'Every time he gave me a piece of jewellery he would say how much he loved me. But his love was as fake as his presents. As fake as he was!'

Russell had to say something. Anything! But his head

was whirling. Nicole wasn't Alistair Power's daughter! Wasn't his enemy's flesh and blood...

He should have been relieved. Instead, he felt shattered.

Desperate to do something, he started the car and accelerated away, scattering some gravel as he did so. He didn't speak till they were idling at their first set of red lights. By then his shock had lessened slightly, but not his overwhelming sense of guilt.

'How old were you when your mother married Alistair Power?'

'Eight.'

'And your real father?'

'I never met him. He was my mother's boss. Married, of course.'

'You've never sought him out?'

'No. He lives in London. With his wife and three sons.'

'Your mother's English?'

'Yes. She had a really tough time of it before she met Alistair. Her parents were extremely old-fashioned and wouldn't have anything to do with her when she had me.'

'So how did she meet Alistair? Did she come out here on a holiday?'

'Oh, no. No, we never had any money for holidays back then. Mum was working for an events organiser in London as a hostess, and Alistair was there on some business trip. They both claim it was love at first sight. Alistair brought Mum and me back to Sydney and they were married in no time flat. Too bad he turned out to be an even bigger bastard than my real father.'

'You're better off without him in your life,' Russell said.

And better without a man like me in your life, too.

'I do know that. Truly I do,' she added. 'But what

about my mother? She's still with him. I'll bet all her jewels are fakes, too. I'll bet Alistair never really loved her, either. She was just a beautiful blonde to have warming his bed and running his house for him.'

'No man marries a woman with a child unless he loves her, Nicole,' Russell said, the concessional words sticking in his throat. But he had to say something to ease her pain, and to soothe her fears.

Besides, it was probably true. There were any number of beautiful blonde bed-mates Power could have chosen to marry, single ones without any emotional or physical baggage.

Yet he'd chosen Nicole's mother.

The lights changed and Russell automatically headed for the city. He wasn't sure where he was going. He was just driving.

'The fake jewels were probably more about money than caring, Nicole,' he told her. 'I gathered from the bank that your stepfather always lived way above his means. He needed every cent he could make, by fair means or foul. That didn't mean he didn't love you, or your mother.'

'He was unfaithful to her,' she said brokenly. 'The same way David was unfaithful to me. Of course, David didn't love me, either,' she finished bitterly, her shoulders sagging, her eyes dropping from his.

Russell could see her spiralling down into a place he knew well, a place full of black despair, followed by the most crippling cynicism. Before he could think better of it he wrenched the car over to the side of the road, jerking on the handbrake then turning to take her startled face in his hands.

'*I* love you,' he said fiercely.

Her still glistening eyes grew wider.

'Do you really? You're not just saying that to make me feel better?'

'I would *die* to make you feel better,' he said. 'But I would not lie to you about something as important as this. I love you, Nicole, and I want you to marry me.'

'*Marry* you! But we've only known each other a few days.'

His hands dropped away but he kept his eyes fastened on hers. 'In a month we'll know each other a lot better.'

'A month,' she repeated, sounding and looking dazed. 'Why a month?'

'That's how long it takes to get a marriage licence. We'll sign all the forms today, then we'll go to Thailand, where I'll help you do whatever it is you want to do there. Will a month be enough to make the changes you want for those kids?'

'I…I guess so.'

'OK. When that month is up, I'll ask you to marry me again.'

She just stared at him. But her eyes had dried. 'I…I don't know what to say.'

'You don't have to say anything.'

He was doing it again, Nicole realised. Sweeping her off her feet, not into his bed this time, but into his life.

Nicole knew she could not afford to make another mistake in her personal life. Today had shown her just how hurt she'd been by what had happened with David and her stepfather. The last few months she'd been running away from that hurt, pretending to herself that she didn't care, that she'd grown up enough to stand on her own two feet.

But when she found out her jewels were fake today,

her underlying vulnerability had hit her. She'd wanted to crawl away somewhere and just cry for a month. Instead, she'd had to come out here and tell Russell the awful truth.

As much as she appreciated his understanding—and his declaration of love—she really wasn't in the right state of mind to make serious decisions about her future. Not now. Not today.

'I'm sorry, Russell,' she said, 'but I do have to say something.'

'Yes?'

'I don't think it's a good idea for you to come to Bangkok with me at all. Not to begin with. No, please don't start arguing with me. Just try to understand. I desperately need some time to myself. To think.'

'About what?'

'About everything. But mostly about my feelings for you.'

'Which are?'

'I don't know any more. I'm not sure I even know me any more. This last weekend… Looking back on it, it doesn't feel real. Everything happened much too quickly.'

'I see…'

'I'm truly sorry. We could keep in touch by phone. Get to know each other better without all the sex getting in the way.'

Russell could not believe the depth of his dismay.

'When do you think I could visit you over there?'

'I'm not sure…'

'And the marriage licence?'

She just shook her head in the negative.

Russell swallowed. He supposed he deserved this after what he'd done. Hugh would not be sympathetic at all.

But he simply could not let this be the end. He loved this woman. And he believed she loved him back. He *had* to believe that, or there was nothing left for him to live for.

'I'm not happy about this,' he ground out through clenched teeth. 'But I'll do what you want.'

'Thank you.'

Don't thank me yet, Russell thought with the same fierce resolve with which he'd sought revenge. I'm not going to let you get away, my darling. Not in a million years!

CHAPTER NINETEEN

NICOLE sat in the shade of a tree, shaking her head in amazement as she watched a group of boys playing football. The day was very hot and very humid, as December days in Bangkok inevitably were.

'Kids have amazing energy, don't they?'

Nicole looked up to see Julie standing a few metres away, a big smile creasing her freckly face.

Julie was English, and of indeterminate age. Possibly fifty. She'd been a nurse back in London. Unmarried and childless, she'd come to Thailand on a working holiday fifteen years ago and never returned to her country of birth.

The locals called her an angel.

'If I'd had more money I could have bought some proper goalposts and nets,' Nicole said, 'but I thought my limited finances were better spent on more essential items.' Although Kara had insisted on giving her a generous five thousand for her jewellery, it hadn't gone all that far. Not when there was so much to be done. The buildings were very run-down.

'You've done wonders,' Julie said. 'Whoops, I think that's your phone ringing. I'll leave you to talk to your boyfriend. It's time I got on with cooking lunch.'

Nicole dived into her hold-all and pulled out her phone, hoping that it *was* Russell. He did ring her every day, but he wasn't the only caller Nicole had. Kara rang fairly often, and so did her mother.

'Hello?' she said.

'Hi there, beautiful.'

'Oh, Russell, I'm so glad it's you and not my mother.' Who'd taken to haranguing Nicole about her decision to return to Bangkok and waste her life there.

'So am I,' Russell said drily.

'Don't tease me.'

'Would I do that?'

'Yes,' she said laughingly. They'd developed a wonderfully relaxed relationship during the three weeks she'd been over here. She'd been so right to come alone, enabling her to get to know Russell better via talking over the phone, without the distraction of all the sexual chemistry between them. She was still inclined to feeling down occasionally when she thought about her stepfather's appalling behaviour, and had had difficulty keeping quiet about the fake jewels when talking to her mother. It had been Russell who'd convinced her not to tell her.

What good would come of breaking her heart? he'd said, showing a soft and sensitive side to his character which she found very endearing. He might be a rich man, but he was nothing like David, or her rotten stepfather.

'So what are you doing today?' Russell asked. 'Painting some more walls?'

'Nope. Not today. It's too hot for that kind of work. I'm just sitting here under a tree, watching the boys play soccer. What are you doing?'

'Not much more than you. It's terribly hot where I am, too.'

'Not as hot as here, I'll bet. How's the house-selling business going?'

'McClain Real Estate is booming, despite the general downturn in the property market. I don't know what's got into my sales people. Perhaps it's my new company rule that they can't work more than a thirty-five-hour week. I've also restructured the sales teams so that married guys with families never work both Saturdays and Sundays. Anyway, the figures for this last month have been fabulous, so much so that my accountant suggested I donate quite a few grand to some worthwhile charity. I know you don't want my money, but I thought your Julie might appreciate a handout. From what you've told me, the orphanage could do with some serious renovating by professional tradesmen. So I was wondering how much that would take. Would a quarter of a million do it, do you think?'

Nicole gasped. 'Did you say a quarter of a million?'

'Not enough? OK, you're a tough negotiator. Make it half a million. Hugh can throw in the other quarter. He's a sucker for donating money to worthy causes.'

'Do you really mean it?'

'Of course I mean it. I never say things I don't mean. Not about money.'

Nicole shot to her feet. 'I'll have to go and tell Julie.'

'Actually no, you don't have to. She already knows.'

'What? How come?'

'Because I just told her myself, a few minutes ago.'

Nicole's head shot round when she realised Russell's voice was coming not just through the phone but from *here*, somewhere nearby.

He was walking towards her across the yard, looking cool and sexy in fawn cargo shorts and a white T-shirt.

'The month isn't up yet,' she said.

'I know.'

He came right up to her, his phone still stuck to his ear, as hers was to her ear.

'I just had to see you,' he said, their eyes locking together. 'Do you want me to leave?'

She shook her head from side to side, unable to speak right at that moment. She'd forgotten the physical effect he had on her. Forgotten the rush of instant hunger which he could evoke simply by looking into her eyes.

'Will you go out to dinner with me tonight?'

She nodded, knowing full well that she'd end up in bed with him afterwards.

He put the phone away and held his hand out towards her. 'I'd like to meet the children now. See what all the fuss is about.'

Russell didn't feel totally confident about his mission till she arrived in the foyer of his hotel that evening at the arranged time, dressed in a very pretty lemon sundress. Her hair was down, falling in a pale curtain down her mostly bare back. Her honey-coloured skin was glowing, her luscious mouth widening into a smile when she saw him.

'I'm sorry I'm not dressed better,' she apologised. 'I don't own any fancy clothes.'

'You look lovely.'

'And you look very sexy,' she returned, looking him up and down.

Bloody hell, Russell thought as he tried to dampen down the wave of heat which flooded his body. It was going to be damned difficult keeping his hands off her all evening.

Hugh had warned him not to rush her, but to wait for the right moment to make his move.

'If things work out you'll have the rest of your lives to be in bed together,' he'd advised him at the airport. 'Be cool.'

Cool. Difficult to be cool when hot blood was roaring around your veins. And when you'd thought of nothing else for the past three weeks but being with the woman you loved.

But Hugh was a savvy guy where the fairer sex was concerned, so Russell just kissed her lightly on the cheek then steered her straight out to the taxi rank in front of the hotel.

The restaurant he'd chosen was not overly lavish or expensive. He knew Nicole didn't go for that kind of thing any more. But it was intimate and romantic, set high on a hill overlooking the city, the alfresco tables dotted around a lush garden which had lots of water features. Their table for two was small, with a single candle in the centre. The menu was strictly Thai food, the wine list made up of mainly Australian wines.

'This is ever so nice,' Nicole said after he'd ordered a bottle of Hunter Valley Chardonnay. 'I'm glad you didn't book some over-the-top à la carte restaurant. I wouldn't feel right about you paying that kind of money for a meal.'

Russell knew that. They'd talked a lot over the past three weeks, which had led to some more preconceptions about her being dismissed. He'd discovered that she hadn't been travelling first class during the months she'd been overseas. She'd backpacked around Europe, her only money her small amount of severance pay from Power Mortgages, where, contrary to his belief, she hadn't held the kind of job where she was privy to company policy.

That money hadn't lasted long. She'd been able to work for a while in England because she had dual citizenship and that had helped her get to Asia. It had been her experiences in Cambodia, and then in Thailand, which had opened her eyes to what real poverty was, completing her transformation from pampered princess to what she called a more socially conscious and compassionate human being.

Russell loved this new part of her nature but wished that, sometimes, she could look at the big picture, instead of focusing on what she saw as wicked extravagances.

'Spending money at expensive restaurants, Nicole, is not a crime,' he pointed out. 'Not when people have the money. Neither is my staying at a five-star hotel. It's good for the world's economy. Good for Thailand's economy because it keeps people in employment.'

She glanced over the table at him, her eyes thoughtful. 'Yes, you're right. I'm in danger of turning into a wowser. There's nothing worse than a reformed sinner, is there?'

'You were never a sinner.'

'I was a blind fool.'

'You were a victim of circumstance. Like we all are,' he mused as he recalled some more of Hugh's parting words.

You can't tell her the truth now, Russ. It's too late. She'll never understand.

He'd agreed, and so had James, who'd been brought up to scratch over the situation when he got back from his honeymoon. The only one left to warn was his mother.

But he'd cross that bridge when he came to it.

If he came to it.

Russell hated that word, if. It haunted him every night.

If only you'd known from the start that she wasn't Power's daughter. If only she'd been someone else entirely. If only you hadn't allowed yourself to become so eaten-up with revenge.

He'd been the blind fool, not Nicole.

Nicole's fingers reaching out to touch his snapped him back to the present.

'Sorry,' he said, and threw her a quick smile.

'What on earth were you thinking about?' she said. 'You looked so sad.'

He was tempted then to take the risk and tell her the truth. Seriously tempted.

But he just couldn't.

'Those kids I met today,' he said instead. 'You were right. They have absolutely nothing.'

'Not for long. Julie was over the moon with your donation.'

'I told her to buy them some toys first and proper beds.'

'She's already put in the orders.'

'Good.'

The wine came at that precise moment. Russell waved aside any pretentious tasting and the waiter poured two full glasses, smiling broadly at them as he settled the bottle in a portable ice bucket next to their table.

After he left, Nicole picked up her glass straight away and took a sip. 'Mmm. This is lovely. I haven't had any wine since…since our weekend together.'

'That seems eons ago,' he said.

'It does, doesn't it?'

The time had come, he decided. He could not wait any longer.

Russell's heart thundered in his chest as he pulled the ring from his pocket.

Nicole knew what he was going to do the second she saw the box.

'This ring is not fake,' he said as he flipped the box open and held it out towards her. 'The emerald is from a famous mine in Columbia. The diamonds are from the Kimberleys. I have a certificate of guarantee for two hundred thousand dollars.'

Nicole stared down at the very beautiful ring, then up at him.

'I'm not trying to buy your love,' he reassured her, 'because I know that's impossible. This is yours no matter what, as a token of my love. My very real love.' He lifted the ring from the box, slipped off his chair and knelt on one knee beside her. 'Will you do me the honour of marrying me, my darling?'

The lump which filled her throat was very real, too. So were the tears which stung her eyes.

Without saying a word, she took the ring from his fingers and slipped it onto her finger. Then she cupped his face and kissed him with a kiss which contained all the love that she was feeling.

His face beamed up at her. 'I take it that's a yes?'

'Yes,' she managed to choke out.

The smiling waiter returned to take their order right at that moment, saw what was happening and let everyone know. The owner of the restaurant—a sweet little old lady—insisted that everything was on the house for them, including the wine. By the time they left, Nicole's head was swimming.

But she was happy. So happy.

'I forgot to tell you that I love you,' she whispered as she snuggled up to Russell in the back of the taxi.

'Could you possibly show me instead?' he whispered back.

'I think I could be persuaded.'

'I love you,' she repeated to him later as they lay wrapped in each other's arms in his hotel room.

'Enough to agree to a wedding before Christmas?'

She levered herself up on one elbow and pushed the hair out of her eyes. 'But Christmas is only three weeks away. You said a marriage licence takes a month.'

'We could get a special licence. Hugh said his father's lawyer could arrange one. He knows all the tricks in the marriage trade.'

She frowned. 'But don't you need a good reason for a special licence?'

Russell shrugged. 'Money opens all doors.'

'It would be nice to be married by Christmas,' she said, thinking that, now she'd made her decision, she didn't want to wait, either.

'You agree?'

'Yes,' she said, and laid her head down on his chest.

Russell started stroking her hair. 'It doesn't give you much time to prepare things,' he said.

'I don't need much time.'

'You're a girl in a million.'

'I certainly am, to have found a wonderful man like you.'

Russell tried not to let guilt raise its ugly head again, but it did. I'm not so wonderful, he almost said.

'I love you,' he whispered.

'I know,' she said with a happy sigh.

CHAPTER TWENTY

'YOU look lovely, sweetie.'

'So do you,' Nicole countered.

'I don't look too bad.' Kara turned to inspect herself in the full-length mirror which hung on the back of her bedroom door. 'It's not to my usual taste. I'd never normally be seen dead in yellow. But Mummy said you asked for yellow and that it was your day so here I am, looking surprisingly good in yellow. But don't worry, I certainly haven't upstaged the bride,' she added, smiling as she pulled Nicole over by her side. 'Now, *that*,' she said, nodding towards Nicole's reflection in the mirror, 'is seriously lovely.'

Nicole had to admit that the ivory silk evening dress she'd bought in Bangkok suited her admirably, the colour complementing her sun-kissed skin, as did the halter-neckline. Although the style was simple, it was classy-looking and elegant, following her very feminine figure before falling in gentle folds from her hips to her ankles.

But it wasn't a proper bridal gown.

Still, she hadn't wanted a big, fancy wedding; hadn't wanted to have what she'd known Alistair would have given her if she'd married David a few months ago. She knew she was probably being a bit silly, but the thought of a sinfully expensive designer dress was anathema to her, not to mention the kind of reception which would have fed the population of a Third World country. Hence the very small guest list and the simple dress, frangipanis adorning her hair instead of the jewel-encrusted tiara and frothy veil that her mother would have chosen for her.

This last thought made Nicole's heart squeeze tight.

Her mother knew she was getting married today, Nicole keeping her up-to-date with her life through phone calls and text messages. The news of her daughter's engagement to Russell had been greeted with surprise and concern at first. But all worry over the speed of their romance had disappeared after Nicole revealed that Russell was wealthy.

Initially her mother said she was coming to the wedding, but Alistair had forbidden it. He'd been worried that certain government officials might find out where he was if his wife returned to Australia. Alistair had finally and grudgingly supplied Nicole with an email address where she could send photos of her special day, testing her earlier resolve never to tell her mother about the fake-jewel fiasco. In the end, Nicole had swallowed her gall, and even emailed a few photos of Megan's wedding so that her mum could at least see what her future son-in-law looked like.

She hadn't had a reply as yet. Hadn't had a phone call today, either. Yet it had just gone four o'clock, the time set down for the ceremony.

'You're thinking about your mum, aren't you?' Kara said with one of her occasional bursts of intuition.

'I thought she might have called me today,' Nicole said, tears pricking at her eyes. 'But she hasn't.'

'Don't you dare start crying!' Kara warned. 'We don't have time to do your make-up again.'

A tap on their door, accompanied by Kara's dad asking if he could come in, had Nicole swiftly blinking away any tears.

'Well, well,' he boomed on seeing them both. 'Don't my two girls look absolutely gorgeous?'

'And so we should,' Kara retorted. 'It's taken us all day to get ready.'

This was true. They'd set off for the beauty salon at eight this morning, only returning just over an hour ago. Nicole had given in to a full range of pampering after Kara presented her with a complimentary gift certificate which the salon had supposedly given to her for being such an excellent customer.

A white lie, Nicole suspected. But it seemed churlish to refuse. And in truth, the experience had been wonderfully relaxing, especially the massage. It had also given her time to lie back and reassess her future lifestyle as Russell's wife.

'If you want to continue with your charitable works,' Russell had stated unequivocally during the flight home from Bangkok, 'then you should join me in my real-estate business. You'd be a great salesperson, with your looks and your personality. That way, you could give away your own money, rather than mine.'

The idea had appealed to her. So had Russell's confidence in her abilities. Of course, she would have to dress the part…

By the time they had finished at the beauty salon, Nicole had resolved to buy some off-the-peg power suits, and to get her hair professionally done at least once a fortnight. The rest, she would do herself.

'Mother suggested you wait up here till you were fashionably late,' Mr Horton said, glancing at his watch, 'but I don't think that's a good idea. The groom is already on the twitchy side,' he directed at Nicole. 'And the best man's not much better.'

Nicole had to smile. She'd got to know Hugh a lot better since returning to Sydney. Got to know James better, too. The two friends had tossed for the privilege of being Russell's best man and Hugh had won again. Or lost, depending on how you looked at it.

Weddings, Hugh had explained over drinks the other night, did not bring out the best in him. Bad memories, caused by his father's many marriages. James had scoffed at this, saying this excuse had whiskers on it and it was about time he grew up.

James was the pragmatic one of the trio, Nicole saw, Hugh the sensitive one. And Russell was the secretive one.

Nicole almost choked on this last thought. Now, where had that come from? She and Russell had no secrets from each other. Russell had always been very open with her, even telling her about his father's suicide, not something any man would relish revealing.

'Let's go, girls,' Mr Horton said.

Nicole gave herself a mental shake and picked up her small bouquet of frangipanis.

'Thank you so much for giving me away, Mr Horton,' she said as the three of them left the room. 'And for letting me have my wedding here.'

'My pleasure, my dear. You've always been a joy to have around. Your Russell is a lucky man.'

'And our Nickie is lucky, too,' Kara piped up as she moved past them to go down the stairs first. 'Now, watch your step. Don't want any last-minute hiccups, do we?'

The staircase was wide and grand, leading down to a black-and-white tiled entrance hall which then led into an elegant dining room on one side and a formal reception room on the other. It was this latter room which Mrs Horton had chosen as the venue for the ceremony and where she'd set up three rows of chairs on either side of a runner of red carpet, at the head of which she'd placed a lectern for the marriage celebrant, borrowed from a minister friend of theirs.

Nicole and Kara had peeped into the room before going upstairs to get ready an hour ago. At that time, the place had been empty and she hadn't felt nervous at all. Now every chair had an occupant and swarms of butterflies quickly gathered in her stomach.

'Don't be nervous,' Mr Horton said, and patted her on the hand. 'Just smile and keep your eyes straight ahead.'

Easier said than done. Impossible not to glance around, especially with Kara right in front of her, blocking her vision of straight ahead. But at least she managed to smile at everyone. Firstly at several of Russell's branch managers with their partners, all of whom she'd met the other night over dinner. Then the Hortons' next-door neighbours, who'd often minded Kara and Nicole when they were children. James and Megan. Kara's boyfriend. Mrs Horton herself.

When she caught the eye of Russell's mother, Nicole's smile froze. The woman didn't look as happy as she had the previous weekend. She'd welcomed Nicole with open arms that day, showing nothing but delight at her son's choice of bride. Today there was tension in her facial muscles, which leapt across the space between them and wound Nicole's stomach even tighter than it already was.

Thankfully, Kara reached the head of the makeshift aisle at that point, moving to the left and giving Nicole an uninterrupted view of the man she'd come to marry.

There was no tension on Russell's face. There was nothing but love. It radiated from his eyes, chasing away her irrational fears and bringing back the warmth in her own smile.

After that, she saw nothing but him till the simple ceremony was over and Russell was kissing her. She did not hear the front door burst open, or the hurried click-clack of high heels across the tiled foyer. She was totally unaware of her mother standing in the doorway of the room, watching them with a horrified look on her face.

Something—some ghastly sixth sense—infiltrated Russell's mind. His mouth jerked up from his bride's, his brain taking a moment to get into gear as his head turned round.

He recognised the woman straight away.

She recognised him, too.

'I'm too late, aren't I?' Nicole's mother croaked out as she stared at him.

Russell didn't say a word. He couldn't. Despair was rising up within him like some hideous beast in a horror movie.

'Mum!' Nicole exclaimed by his side in the happiest voice. 'You came!'

Cold green eyes speared him. 'She has no idea, has she?'

Nicole glanced up at him, her forehead wrinkling into a puzzled frown. 'No idea about what?'

'You poor darling,' her mother said as she walked towards them. 'You think he loves you, don't you?'

A collective gasp reverberated around the room.

Nicole's fingers tightened around her husband's. 'Russell *does* love me.'

'Tell her. Tell her the truth.'

'The truth is I *do* love her,' Russell said, steeling himself for the fight of his life. 'Nicole is the love of my life.'

'Liar!' The vicious word echoed in the now silent room. 'I thought it was you as soon as I saw your photo. But I couldn't be sure. I had to come and see for myself. Alistair said you couldn't possibly be the same boy. But you most definitely are. I've never forgotten your eyes, or the hate I saw burning in them that day. You would have killed Alistair if I hadn't stopped you.'

Nicole lifted a shocked face to his. 'Russell, what is Mum talking about?'

'I'm talking about revenge,' the woman swept on before he could voice any defence. 'Your new husband held Alistair responsible for his father's suicide. Something to do with Power Mortgages repossessing the family property. He vowed he would get even with Alistair one day. Vowed to take everything Alistair held dear. You yourself told me he bought our place in Belleview Hill.'

'Which I have already sold,' Russell broke in.

'Only after you found a better revenge. You are not the love of his life, my darling daughter. You are his bride of vengeance.'

Nicole wasn't the only one in the room to suck in sharply.

'Ask him!' her mother demanded. 'Ask him to tell you the truth right now in front of everyone. If he really does love you, then the truth should hold no fear for him.'

Once again, Nicole looked up at him. 'Russell?'

'It's not his fault!'

Everyone in the room stared at the man who'd spoken.

'He wanted to tell you the truth right from the start,' Hugh added as he strode round to take Nicole's hands in his, 'but I talked him out of it. I said it was a risk he didn't need to take. No one else knew about that ancient history, except for me and James and his mother. And it was easy to get the others to keep quiet. But I never thought of *your* mum, dear Nicole. You have to believe Russ. He really loves you.'

Russell was touched by Hugh's truly gallant gesture, but he could not let his good friend take the fall for him.

It was time for the truth, warts and all.

'Nice try, Hugh,' he said, and squeezed his shoulder, 'but Nicole deserves the total truth.' He turned her to face him so that she could look into his eyes and hopefully see for herself that he wasn't lying. 'Initially, I did entertain the thought of getting some kind of revenge through you. I was angry that Alistair had escaped overseas and not faced justice for what he'd done. Buying his house hadn't satisfied me. I needed more. When we first met, I mistakenly thought you were his flesh-and-blood daughter...'

She continued to stare up at him, her eyes searching his as he relayed what had to be the most hurtful facts.

'Hugh was appalled by my trying to use you as a weapon of vengeance. He threatened to tell you the truth that night we had dinner together at Neptune's. But I made him promise not to breathe a word. He wasn't happy about it but I convinced him that silence was the lesser of two evils. I told him that the truth would break your heart, which was the last thing I wanted. Because by then, my darling, I was already falling in love with you.'

Nicole remembered that night well, remembered the false conclusions she'd jumped to over Hugh's behaviour.

It hadn't been Hugh who'd been the villain on that occasion. It had been Russell, the man she loved, the man she'd just married. Russell, who'd seduced her out of revenge, in her own mother's bed.

She should have been appalled. So why wasn't she?

'I know what I did was unforgivable,' he went on, his eyes carrying that sadness which she'd sometimes glimpsed in them. 'I've had great difficulty forgiving myself. But I do love you, Nicole, with a love so strong that it transcended revenge. Trust me when I say that has to be a very great love, because the thought of revenge sustained me for sixteen years. I lived and breathed it. But then you came along and soon I didn't want revenge any more. I just wanted…you.'

Nicole's heart turned over at the tender emotion in his voice, at the cracking in his voice. What he'd done was wrong. Yes, very wrong. But perfectly understandable. If she'd been in his place she might have done the same. As she stared up into Russell's tortured face she saw the truth as it stood today. He did love her. Everything else was past history. Everything else was irrelevant.

'I *do* love you, my darling,' he insisted. 'And I'm so very, very sorry. I will understand, however, if you don't want anything more to do with me,' he added with a weary sigh. 'I'm sure an annulment could be arranged. It's up to you.'

There was hushed silence in the room, everyone waiting with bated breath to hear what she was going to say.

'I'm sorry, too,' she said, 'that you didn't feel you

could tell me all this earlier. Because it makes absolutely no difference to me why and how we got together. I know you love me as much as I love you.'

When he stared down at her she smiled up at him.

'Don't be such a blind fool!' her mother exclaimed.

'That's enough from you!' Nicole snapped, her eyes whipping round to her mother. 'You stood by a man who's done much worse than my Russell. I will not have another word spoken against my husband. We love each other and that is all that matters here today.'

'Absolutely,' came a girl's voice.

It was Megan who stood up and began to clap. Sweet shy Megan.

Nicole would be eternally grateful to her.

Everyone else followed, standing up and clapping. Even her mother, who looked chastened by her daughter's blunt words.

'Would you mind if I kissed you again?' Russell whispered to Nicole.

She didn't mind one bit.

Russell closed his eyes as his lips met hers. Closed his eyes to everything but what this beautiful girl could make him feel.

Love.

Nicole was so right. It was all that mattered…

* * * * *

Turn the page for an exclusive extract from:
THE SHEIKH'S FORBIDDEN VIRGIN
by
Kate Hewitt

Taken by the sheikh for pleasure—but as his bride…?

At her coming-of-age at twenty-one, Kalila is pledged to marry the Calistan king. Scarred, sexy Sheikh Prince Aarif is sent to escort her, his brother's betrothed, to Calista. But when the willful virgin tries to escape, he has to catch her, and the desert heat leads to scorching desire—a desire that is forbidden!

Aarif claims Kalila's virginity—even though she can never be his! Once she comes to walk up the aisle on the day of her wedding, Kalila's heart is in her mouth: *who is waiting to become her husband at the altar?*

A LIGHT, INQUIRING KNOCK SOUNDED on the door, and, turning from that grim reminder, Aarif left the bathroom and went to fulfill his brother's bidding, and express his greetings to his bride.

The official led him to the double doors of the Throne Room; inside, an expectant hush fell like a curtain being dropped into place, or perhaps pulled up.

"Your Eminence," the official said in French, the national language of Zaraq, his voice low and unctuous, "may I present His Royal Highness, King Zakari."

Aarif choked; the sound was lost amid a ripple of murmurings from the palace staff, who had assembled for this honored occasion. It would take King Bahir only one glance to realize it was not the king who graced his Throne Room today, but rather the king's brother, a lowly prince.

Aarif felt a flash of rage—directed at himself. A mistake had been made in the correspondence, he supposed. He'd delegated the task to an aide when he should have written himself and explained that he would be coming rather than his brother.

Now he would have to explain the mishap in front of

company—all of Bahir's staff—and he feared the insult could be great.

"Your Eminence," he said, also speaking French, and moved into the long, narrow room with its frescoed ceilings and bare walls. He bowed, not out of obeisance but rather respect, and heard Bahir shift in his chair. "I fear my brother, His Royal Highness Zakari, was unable to attend to this glad errand, due to pressing royal business. I am honored to escort his bride, the princess Kalila, to Calista in his stead."

Bahir was silent, and, stifling a prickle of both alarm and irritation, Aarif rose. He was conscious of Bahir watching him, his skin smooth but his eyes shrewd, his mouth tightening with disappointment or displeasure, perhaps both.

Yet even before Bahir made a reply, even before the formalities had been dispensed with, Aarif found his gaze sliding, of its own accord, to the silent figure to Bahir's right.

It was his daughter, of course. Kalila. Aarif had a memory of a pretty, precocious child. He'd spoken a few words to her at the engagement party more than ten years ago now. Yet now the woman standing before him was lovely, although, he acknowledged wryly, he could see little of her.

Her head was bowed, her figure swathed in a kaftan, and yet, as if she felt the magnetic tug of his gaze, she lifted her head and her eyes met his.

It was all he could see of her, those eyes; they were almond-shaped, wide and dark, luxuriously fringed, a deep, clear golden brown. Every emotion could be seen in them, including the one that flickered there now as her gaze was drawn inexorably to his face, to his scar.

It was disgust Aarif thought he saw flare in their golden depths, and as their gazes held and clashed he felt a sharp, answering stab of disappointment and self-loathing in his own gut.

* * * * *

Be sure to look for
THE SHEIKH'S FORBIDDEN VIRGIN
by Kate Hewitt,
available October from Harlequin Presents®!

TWO CROWNS, TWO ISLANDS, ONE LEGACY

A royal family torn apart by pride and its lust for power, reunited by purity and passion

THE ROYAL HOUSE *of* KAREDES

Look for the next passionate adventure in
The Royal House of Karedes:

THE SHEIKH'S FORBIDDEN VIRGIN
by Kate Hewitt, October 2009

THE GREEK BILLIONAIRE'S INNOCENT PRINCESS
by Chantelle Shaw, November 2009

THE FUTURE KING'S LOVE-CHILD
by Melanie Milburne, December 2009

RUTHLESS BOSS, ROYAL MISTRESS
by Natalie Anderson, January 2010

THE DESERT KING'S HOUSEKEEPER BRIDE
by Carol Marinelli, February 2010

www.eHarlequin.com

HP12859

*When a wealthy man takes a wife,
it's not always for love…*

Miranda Lee

presents the next installment in the
Three Rich Husbands trilogy

THE BILLIONAIRE'S BRIDE OF CONVENIENCE

Book #2860

Available October 2009

Find out why Russell, Hugh and James, three wealthy
Sydney businessmen, don't believe in marrying for love,
and how this is all about to change….

Pick up the last passionate story
from this fabulous trilogy,

**THE BILLIONAIRE'S
BRIDE OF INNOCENCE**

November 2009

www.eHarlequin.com

HP12860

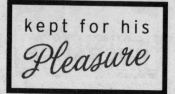

HARLEQUIN *Presents*

EXTRA

DARK NIGHTS WITH
A BILLIONAIRE

*Untamed, commanding—
and impossible to resist!*

Swarthy and scandalous, dark and dangerous, these
brooding billionaires are used to keeping women for as
many nights as they want, and then discarding them....

But when they meet someone who throws their best-laid
plans off track, will these imposing, irrepressible men
be brought to their knees by love?

**Catch all of the books in this fabulous
Presents Extra collection, available October 2009:**

The Venetian's Midnight Mistress #73
by CAROLE MORTIMER

Kept for Her Baby #74
by KATE WALKER

Proud Revenge, Passionate Wedlock #75
by JANETTE KENNY

Captive In the Millionaire's Castle #76
by LEE WILKINSON

REQUEST YOUR FREE BOOKS!

HARLEQUIN *Presents*

2 FREE NOVELS PLUS 2
FREE GIFTS!

PASSION
GUARANTEED
SEDUCTION

YES! Please send me 2 FREE Harlequin Presents® novels and my 2 FREE gifts (gifts are worth about $10). After receiving them, if I don't wish to receive any more books, I can return the shipping statement marked "cancel." If I don't cancel, I will receive 6 brand-new novels every month and be billed just $4.05 per book in the U.S. or $4.74 per book in Canada. That's a savings of close to 15% off the cover price! It's quite a bargain! Shipping and handling is just 50¢ per book*. I understand that accepting the 2 free books and gifts places me under no obligation to buy anything. I can always return a shipment and cancel at any time. Even if I never buy another book, the two free books and gifts are mine to keep forever.

106 HDN EYRQ 306 HDN EYR2

Name	(PLEASE PRINT)	
Address		Apt. #
City	State/Prov.	Zip/Postal Code

Signature (if under 18, a parent or guardian must sign)

Mail to the Harlequin Reader Service:
IN U.S.A.: P.O. Box 1867, Buffalo, NY 14240-1867
IN CANADA: P.O. Box 609, Fort Erie, Ontario L2A 5X3

Not valid to current subscribers of Harlequin Presents books.

Are you a current subscriber of Harlequin Presents books and want to receive the larger-print edition? Call 1-800-873-8635 today!

* Terms and prices subject to change without notice. Prices do not include applicable taxes. Sales tax applicable in N.Y. Canadian residents will be charged applicable provincial taxes and GST. Offer not valid in Quebec. This offer is limited to one order per household. All orders subject to approval. Credit or debit balances in a customer's account(s) may be offset by any other outstanding balance owed by or to the customer. Please allow 4 to 6 weeks for delivery. Offer available while quantities last.

Your Privacy: Harlequin Books is committed to protecting your privacy. Our Privacy Policy is available online at www.eHarlequin.com or upon request from the Reader Service. From time to time we make our lists of customers available to reputable third parties who may have a product or service of interest to you. If you would prefer we not share your name and address, please check here. ☐

HP09R

I ♥

HARLEQUIN *Presents*

BROUGHT TO YOU BY FANS OF
HARLEQUIN PRESENTS.

We are its editors and authors
and biggest fans—and we'd
love to hear from YOU!

Subscribe today to our online blog at
www.iheartpresents.com